Tangy Bonanza by Doc Solammen
has been published in an edition of 352 copies
offered for sale in the following manner:

A fifty-two copy, signed & lettered,
limited edition hardcover.

A three hundred copy, signed & numbered,
limited edition trade paperback.

Doc Solammen

145

DOC SOLAMMEN

ORLANDO • 2001

DOC SOLAMMEN

PASTE

first edition

"Tangy Bonanza"
©2001 by Doc Solammen
"Tryptophan"
©2001 by Doc Solammen

cover & interior art ©2001 Chris Trammell

this edition September 2001 © Bedlam Press

book design & typesetting:
David G. Barnett
faT caT Design
PO BOX 540298
Orlando, FL 32854-0298

assistant editor:
John Everson
Jeffrey Thomas

a Bedlam Press book
PO Box 540298
Orlando, FL 32854-0298
Bedlam Press is an imprint of Necro Publications.

trade paperback ISBN: 1-889186-19-8
hardcover ISBN: 1-889186-20-1

For Richard...who saved us.

The individuals alluded to in this work are real—
May God forgive them...and me for loving them.
                                                    —D.S.

Chapter 1

Abstinence, Rehab, and Chamber Music

I sit across the expansive dining room table waiting for the dog to make his move. He stares back at me with passive almond eyes and tilts his head to catch the scent of my Scotch. He's trying to be subtle, but I'm on to him. The arrogant son of a bitch fancies himself a connoisseur of liquors and is endeavoring to ascertain whether or not I'm drinking the *Glenlevit* he proudly presented me on my 34th birthday, or if I'm back to my staple *Cutty Sark*, which he condescendingly regards as swill.

I'm growing nervous. The glass *is* filled with *Cutty Sark* and I know how Bro can be when he feels slighted. Weeks of bowel control problems could ensue if I dodn't play this just right. I turn the bottle—which I stupidly brought to the breakfast table—so the yellow label with its namesake maritime insignia is out of the dog's line of sight.

I once caught the animal red-handed using my American Express card and a bootleg cellular telephone, trying to order the *Hooked on Phonics* material. I don't think he ever received it. I canceled the card. One can't be too careful, though. If the beast has learned to read, I'm fucked. He already suspects I'm feeding him a senior dog food instead of his beloved *Alpo*, and if he should somehow (God forbid) discover this and my numerous other acts of paternal "misdirection" which are, after all, only a semester's worth of reading comprehension away, I'll have to shoot him dead.

Bro is old now. Somewhere in the geriatric throes of his

canine seventies and the arthritis is twisting him up. I hear him sometimes in the early morning howling out his ineffectual protests against the disease's debilitating progress. I love nothing more than to slap my palm against his door and tell him to "Rage! Rage against the dying of the light!" More often then not he snarls back a string of curses which, were it not for the shortcomings of his palette and his resultant inability to enunciate complex diphthongs such as the "Aay-owr" in, *I'm going to dog-fuck your aorta after I gnaw through your sternum and dig your heart out*, would shock and horrify a south Chicago social worker.

It became obvious after some years that the disease was disintegrating Bro's body with such ferocity that his mind was also slipping and breaking up in the tumultuous waves of pain. Some days I would wake up and fix the two of us mimosas, only to have them go flat waiting for Bro to come to the breakfast table. Upon finally being forced to go down to his bedroom, I would find him lying naked, torn out of his flannel pajamas, massaging *Ben-Gay* into his pelvis. Seeing me he would implore me to fetch pen and paper that he might dictate his final will and testament, so convinced was he that he would expire in the relentless path of the disease. Thus far, the animal has bequeathed unto me the greater part of my own property, which he mistakenly presumes to be his own. He claims, in his ignorance of civil law, to be the rightful owner of the house and lands, owing to the fact that, unlike me, who must leave the estate to work in the real world, he is a perennial fixture on the grounds. Sufficient coaxing would, in most cases, rouse Bro from his morning agonies. Two quarts of orange juice and a bottle of some expensive champagne of his choosing later, his spirits would be sufficiently improved for him to engage in civil conversation.

My withers are a fucking mess and my flanks are a damnable agony. Whole Goddamn pelvis feels like it's made of low-grade ceramic. I'm afraid that if I stumble into the toilet or knock my ass against a door frame it'll shatter, and after a month of passing porcelain shards and rectal bleeding, I'll settle into a deplorable life of dragging my useless hindquarters behind me like some foul, excrement-leaking duffel bag. What's more, you'll probably have me put to sleep for soiling your blasé shag carpeting, you ruthless cock sucker. This mimosa is pure shit...entirely second rate. The champagne is dying in this...what is this anyway? Orange juice? Christ, I can't even drink my orange juice in the morning anymore without a couple of shots of vodka in it. Let's have Bloody Marys instead.

I agree and inventory our tomato juice, olive, Worcestershire sauce, celery, and Tabasco stocks. Bro, in the meantime, has had misgivings about the cheese omelets I've prepared for breakfast. He claims eggs and cheese together are an evil analogy for biological reproduction, given their origins, and refuses to eat them on the principal that he, although entirely unaltered, (I would never subject him to what must most surely be the *horror* of castration), has led a celibate life because of my insensitivities to his needs and long-standing refusal to provide him with a concubine.

Let's go out for breakfast today, he muses. *I think pancakes would go down nicely. Don't you?*

I agree and twenty minutes later we board the stylish '74 Cadillac Coupe Deville convertible I own, along with a bevy of equally stunning specimens of prime Detroit iron. CD player blasting Black Sabbath's "Into the Void," we lurch in a great and glorious tribute to unadulterated displacement out into the arterial mess of West Seattle's civil engineering shortcomings. Music is one of the few subjects upon which Bro and I agree. The works of Black Sabbath, Iron Maiden, Ronnie James Dio, Rainbow, Judas Priest, AC/DC, Rush, Triumph, Led Zeppelin and the Who represent the vast majority of our collective and unparalleled recording library. One of my ex-girlfriends, a member of an elitist society whose ranks continue to swell, once slandered the masterful, adrenaline instigating vocals of Iron Maiden's Bruce Dickinson. Hot in the middle of "Children of the Damned" she erringly commented that the noise pouring from my monolithic home entertainment village was "Inappropriate for what was *supposed to be* a romantic evening."

Unbeknownst to me at the time, but no mystery to Bro, was the fact that this comely, if not cultured, lass was down in the bloody trenches of a memorable menstrual episode and had already left a shrewdly embalmed tampon interred deep in my toilet side trash receptacle. Bro, having taken serious offense to the unfortunate shortcomings in the young lady's musical tastes, left the front room and reappeared some moments later with the aforementioned soiled tampon dangling merrily from his slobbering jowls. He approached us, the girl in particular, and to her scarcely restrained shock and revulsion, chewed vigorously upon and then ate the nasty morsel.

Her voice quivered with embarrassment and anger as she excused herself. I was quite sure she was weeping as she slammed herself into the impeccably clean confines of her Volkswagen Cabriolet convertible and disappeared in a flurry of Depeche Mode's monotonic ramblings. The dog and I watched her dramatic departure intently. I, with mild disappointment, and he, with mild curiosity.

"You had to do that, didn't you?" I had been reduced to rhetoric.

It isn't like the damn thing tasted good, he countered. *Hell, I need a drink. Are we down on scotch? How about a Rusty Nail? Can you pull that Drambuie down from the pantry? Thanks.*

Chapter 2

Physicians, Attorneys, Morphine, and Manslaughter

T he community that sprung up around the Seattle-Tacoma International Airport had, in the early '90s, demanded and won autonomy. The newly founded city of "Sea-Tac" began immediately to abuse its legislative authority by passing a law which required all establishments of a "carnal" nature lying within the city's limits to diminish the artistic potential of their erotic dancers by encumbering them with G-strings. For this very reason, Bro and I seldom venture into that puritanical city state unless we are forced to do so.

This was one of those instances. The Pancake Chef is a breakfast eatery of unequaled excellence. Piping hot stacks of obscenely delicious hot cakes are dispensed at a positively hazardous pace from sun-up until early afternoon. One quickly learns to disregard the syrup smattered floor and its associated hazards and ease into a blissful "Who gives a shit if we're in Sea-Tac" frame of mind while gorging himself to a gastric point of no return from which no amount of antacid therapy can provide deliverance. Before the hostess could voice protest about my bringing a dog into the establishment, I loudly demanded a table for "Scirocco and *son*." I stared a brazen challenge at the woman, daring her to call unnecessary and embarrassing attention to my son's infirmities.

She grudgingly showed us to our booth which was, not surprisingly, removed some distance from the greater body of diners and presented us with huge, laminated menus.

"I'll have a pot of coffee, two glasses of sugar on the

side and a bowl of nonfat milk to start with. My son will have a shallow tin of coagulated bacon grease and a Bloody Mary. What's that? You don't serve cocktails? Oh. In that case bring him a glass of iced tomato juice, a bottle of Tabasco, some garlic salt, a dash of black pepper, some fennel seeds, two pimento stuffed olives in about a tablespoon of olive juice, some Worcestershire sauce, a celery stalk and two ounces of Draino. Thank you."

She was about to say something which would, no doubt, have hampered our enjoyment of the casual, late-morning ambiance, but thought better of it and shuffled off, scratching out an order she hoped somebody would understand. Good thing, too. Just as she disappeared through the dangerously heavy looking and wildly swinging kitchen door, Bro was wracked by a nasty bout of "arthritis shivers." He contorted like a 75-pound cramp and began chanting some moronic mantra he'd memorized during a period of *Sesame Street* viewing which had marked his earliest attempt at literacy.

I leapt up from my vinyl couch and gestured wildly for help. I maintained an inner composure, however, and even as I ascended the table and doused those unfortunate, apathetic few in close proximity to our little family tragedy with lemony ice water, I was scanning the crowd for a doctor. At the extreme opposite end of the dining area, I spied a middle-aged man with that hint of gray at the temples which suggested that his practice was really beginning to take off. I once knew a doctor who claimed that the best thing ever to have befallen his long mediocre practice was a bit of timely graying at his temples. Old people, who constituted the bulk of his patient load (he was a vascular surgeon) suddenly identified with him and felt him more qualified to go dredging through their wilted chest cavities on an obscene, plaque-purging witch hunt. I locked eyes with the deceptive doctor and he, feeling himself discovered, produced from beneath his chair a handsome medical bag and began to push his way across the agitated room. There was no tricking this learned man of medicine about my son's biological lineage so I didn't even try. I blurted out the entire, unattractive truth: how Bro had been sired by Mister Ed and how the legendary dam, Lassie, had eaten his fourteen litter mates so as to grant him unrestricted rights to all ten of her nutrient spurting teats. I explained how Bro had grown in leaps and bounds until 1986 when he had been poisoned by Annheiser Busch operatives who put arthritis pellets into his *Whiskas* (he had gone through a phase in the late '80s during which he thought cat food chic—a deviation from the mean.) The corporate assassins had doomed him to a life of embittered cripppledness because he had flatly refused to appear in a string of *Budweiser* commercials in which he was to run alongside and make lunatic passes through the galloping hooves of a team of dauntingly enormous horses.

Bro's attorney at the time, a south Chicago polack who had emigrated to Seattle on a Suzuki GS-850 in the dying months of 1980, had advised him *not* to accept the contract on the premise that it was unsafe for the son and heir to the Mister Ed fortune to mingle with obviously violent, equine semi-contemporaries who could, after all, be family. Nothing, he advised, could be uglier than slighted half brothers out for a cut of the fortune of an indiscriminate spiller of thoroughbred semen as was Mister Ed. He had reputedly cavorted with all of the Hollywood heavies of the time, including an aging Mae West who, after spending a particularly spirited evening with the virile Ed, had insisted to her production company that the title of her long popular comedy caper *The Bank Dick* be changed to something suggestive of a tribute to the celebrated stallion. Now, ten years worth of regrets later, here we were, Bro twitching and drooling in unmitigated panic as a reluctant vascular surgeon eased a needle dripping pharmaceutical morphine into his crippled withers, while I frantically whipped up a "Draino Mary" more for myself than the dog.

The morphine seemingly did Bro more good than my concoction did me. The waves of pain that had broken his otherwise handsome features into a collage of misery had subsided and the effect was marvelous. Bro looked young again and at peace with the world. He visibly relaxed against the good doctor's thigh and lazily licked his lips as the drug bore him ever deeper into the pulpy recesses of his own private and blissfully pain free paradise.

"Lots of sleep and maybe some heavy drooling for the next twelve hours or so but after that he'll be fine," the doctor advised. "What he really needs is a *veterinarian*."

The old hostess had hovered just outside the closed knot of curious onlookers and her head snapped violently at the doctor's implication that my beloved son was perhaps, as she had suspected all along, a dog. I had to act fast to take the flatulence out of her polyester sails. I lunged at the well-meaning physician and, seizing him by the lapels, screamed so everyone within a two-block radius would hear, "A veterinarian? How dare you sir? And you call yourself a doctor. How do I know you really *are* a doctor? That you're not some career night school under-achiever with a head full of grand designs and a satchel full of cut-rate poisons you whipped up over a Bunsen burner in your mother's basement and dispense under the guise of emergency medication?"

This display had an immediate and remarkably dramatic effect. The crowd, too stunned to act on any of the dozens of knee-jerk notions or raw emotions wracking their haggard ranks, parted nicely as I gathered my opiate pacified son from the puddle of drool he had been manufacturing and tore, like a mad man, toward the parking lot and the promise of safety the great Cadillac held.

"Hey, mister! What about the bill?" It seemed the only person of enduring sensibilities was our own waitress who had probably realized at the last moment that if we didn't pay the modest tab, she would have to. Theft wasn't exactly new to me and I elected to proceed with maximum speed and minimal comment away from this evil little scene and resume a normal existence far, far away from the wretched city of Sea-Tac. My son, roused by the rude jarring and rush of fresh air, stirred in my arms, smiled approvingly and croaked out a few lines of "Knocking on Heaven's Door." *Wonderful*, I thought. *I'm a felon on the lam from the Sea-Tac breakfast squad and the Goddamn stupid, stoned dog is mutating into an overly handsome facsimile of Bob Dylan.*

"Stop! What about the bill?" The waitress was following us now, relentless. Oh, the bitch! Evil, evil little cunt. Young, too, and probably fast. Had to stay ahead of her. Horror now! The dog had heard her. He twisted in my grasp and came perilously close to dislodging himself and falling to an ugly death on the oily asphalt. The effort taxed him beyond his endurance. Bro slipped from consciousness and, as he did so, let loose an abhorrent torrent of canine excrement. The pursuing waitress lost her footing in the offal and took an ugly fall. Jingle of keys and screech of expensive rubber. In the rear view mirror a dwindling scene of concerned "do-gooders" milled around the fallen waitress. The silver fox doctor emerged and turned toward us and the cresting sun. He drew a syringe full of morphine for the injured girl. It had already been a busier day than he was hoping for.

None of this was good. No, not good at all. The time seemed right for legal advice. I pulled the cell phone from its holster and punched the pre-programmed speed dial button which would get my attorney on the line, stat. A man of my position and influence operates in a legally hazardous environment. An attorney of inscrutable character and unblemished reputation, held on exorbitantly expensive retainer is not only a necessity but, in my social circle, a status symbol.

I had no such person. I had something better. I had a filthy animal, an incalculably shrewd, unwaveringly heartless and altogether *evil*—in a word "perfect"—Attorney at Law. I had Jonny. Jonny S. had graduated from Indiana

University's northwest extension in beautiful *Gary*. He was an unflinching racist who would have called Farrakhan a "nigger" to his face and then sued him for "unequal representation" in the million man march. Jonny held the fictitious serial killer, Dr. Hannibal Lecter, in the highest esteem and brought his hero's cold, manipulative genius to the courtroom. In all the years I had utilized Jonny's services, he had lost only one case. That was an anomaly in which the jury took pity on and pardoned a homeless schizophrenic woman who had inadvertently wandered into one of my restaurants and made off with a shopping cart full of expensive knives.

Jonny argued with a zeal, more like that of the street corner Jesus than the educated attorney, that the woman was *dangerous*—a nomadic psychopath with an eye for Chicago Cutlery who was no doubt butchering and living on the raw flesh of Catholic children who rode the bus from Magnolia into downtown Seattle for the purpose of attending parochial school. He paid off and then called a veritable "who's who" of waterfront vagrants to testify against the accused (who, herself, sat silent and motionless throughout the whole of the proceedings, rising only once to proclaim to the Judge, a gaunt man of some 70 years, that the space beneath his robe and between his legs was filled with stinging bees, and that his only chance for survival was to call a recess and leap, naked, from his seventh story window).

Bums from across Seattle, men whose names were a mystery even to themselves, testified against the kleptomaniacal bag lady. In the interest of credibility, Jonny provided them names. No one, with the exception of myself and Jonny, reacted with any hint of alarm when the bailiff called the likes of "Sterno Sam," "Harry Pitts," and "Jim Shoe" to the stand. Mr. Shoe, when instructed to place his right hand on the Bible and swear the oath of honesty, produced from his pocket an evil-looking metal claw. The bailiff apologized and instructed Mr. Shoe to place his left hand on the book instead. An equally hideous metallic appendage emerged from the left pocket as well. After a brief conference, His Honor and both councils agreed to allow the unfortunate Mr. Shoe to testify so long as he *sat* on the Bible while doing so.

Sadly, the vagrants proceeded to give all manner of disjointed, largely contradictory testimony. The judge threw the case out and fined Jonny $1,000 for "frivolous professional misconduct." Six weeks later Jonny took a short vacation during which the body of the bag lady was found bristling with cruel blades, rolling lazily in a shopping cart under the Alaskan Way viaduct. The incident merited little formal police involvement and, aside from a brief, page six article in the *Post Intelligencer*, went largely unnoticed. Jonny returned to work in much improved spirits.

So it was that, once again, I hit the "hot button" and prepared to loose the dogs of modern war. Jonny answered, as always, on the second ring. "Yha, Boss."

"Jonny, can you be at number one in half an hour?"

"Sure... Do I need Helen?"

Helen was Jonny's paralegal. A statuesque redhead fresh out of the University of Washington with whom Jonny seemed genuinely enamored, which is to say he hadn't yet sodomized her, but was getting close.

"No. Just you on this one."

"Yha, sure. See you there."

Chapter 3

How Did We Get Here Anyway?

In 1987, I stepped from a Continental Airlines Airbus 300 through a refreshingly cold and damp jet-way into the buzz of Seattle's cultural rhythm, a daunting and far cry from the paranoia and pessimism of my native Chicago. The Jet City rolled in a syncopated groove that rose and subsided in intensity so much like the perpetual rains for which the region is famous. I am a great lover of rain and of overcast skies and of inclement weather of any sort. The tightly drawn confines of a blustery, storm-ridden day bring about in me a feeling of community, a sense of being stuck, so to speak, in a shared hardship with my fellow man. The fact that I do, for the most part, despise my fellow man in no way effects this feeling.

It was, nonetheless, my fellow man, Jonny (barely out of law school and a semi-dangerous reveler in illegal pharmaceuticals at the time of our introduction) who encouraged and supported me in the enterprise that ultimately raised the two of us from the ranks of the working poor to the precipice of gross excess and lewd debauchery we enjoy today. A severely condensed account of those pivotal days would read as follows:

May, 1988: Jonny and I leave the workplace, a prefabricated home design and distribution firm, and proceed at breakneck speed in my light-blue Renault station wagon through the streets of south Seattle. The late hour and our desire to acquire hard drink before the state-owned liquor stores close necessitates haste. A rush of gym shoes and a rustle of cash later, a fifth of Cutty Sark and pint of Yukon Jack clank merrily together in the back seat. Guitars and a frightening assortment of no-nonsense amplification gear force the little car down low on its suspension as we continue northward on I-5, toward 45th and the University District.

On the corner of 55th and Roosevelt stood an inauspicious automotive service facility. Its hand-painted signage read "Honda Master." It was in front of this most unlikely of buildings that we stopped and began to unload the car. I produced a key and slid it expertly into the prehistoric deadbolt of the building's inconspicuous side entrance, and groped for the light switch. High overhead, a single, bare, incandescent bulb hissed to life, illuminating the wooden stairs that led down into the musty recesses of a long-failed recording studio that served as our rehearsal space.

We, Jonny and I, were rock musicians, and along with a drummer and alleged vocalist whose names are irrelevant, comprised a hard-driving quartet known in those dark days as Iniquity. The subterranean echo chamber in which we congregated for the dark purpose of worshipping the "Metal God" was predictably dubbed, *The Den of Iniquity.*

Music flowed out from us and alcohol flowed in. By rehearsal's end, Jonny and I were crazy with liquor and set out to find something cleaner—some pharmaceutical, meticulously extracted from obscure plants or extinct animals—to elevate us to that intangible plateau just beyond alcohol's powers of transport. We agreed that the night's budget of $25 would prove adequate and walked 200 yards south of the den, stopping in front of a popular collegiate night spot ominously christened, Dante's. Grotesque effigies of Satan himself leered from the establishment's medieval facade, and together with the glowing red fixtures that constituted the entirety of the pub's interior lighting, created a wonderfully seedy atmosphere—the perfect backdrop for the type of low-level, criminal behavior in which Jonny and I had come to engage.

Jan

Jan was a student at The University of Washington. A friend of a friend, if you will, she and I had known one another for some time. Her husband, Leon, a strange but likable chap, was an enlisted man in the Navy and seldom local. Navy policy strictly forbade recreational drug use and, to that end, a program of random testing, unparalleled in the civilian world, had been implemented by whatever ruling body governs that proud organization. Seamen with cruel predispositions for contraband intoxicants had, by reason of brute necessity, ascended to a level of covertness revered by the rest of the drug culture. Marijuana, cocaine, heroin, speed—all of these could be easily detected by standard means of testing. Acid, on the other hand, could not.

A distinction needs be drawn at this point. LSD, the original, highly touted hallucinogen, was no longer realistically attainable. Variations on LSD's theme, insidious, strychnine-based poisons brewed by chemistry dropouts, had replaced their venerable ancestor in the black market menu of the late '80s. These contemporary marvels could be had in either traditional blotter or a more elegant tablet form.

Jan, via her connections with Leon, was an inexhaustible source of the latter. She peddled her wares for $3 a hit from a front table at Dante's. Recognizing us immediately, she invited Jonny and me to join her in a pitcher of pilsner. Pitchers of domestic beer could be had for $2 on Thursdays and, as luck would have it, Thursday had dawned some 22 hours prior.

"Hi, Jan," I lasciviously smiled. "You are one fabulous looking woman. Still married? Too bad. Do you still fantasize about fucking a wolf? I want to see that if it should come to pass. Do for us? Well, we need some setting up, if you take my meaning. Can you help? You can. Great. Price still the same? No, that's not necessary. We'll pay the going rate. Twenty-five bucks worth is what we need. Do you have that much? Good, good. Of course, that blows our wad, which means beer is on you."

We sat to either side of Jan on a bench seat facing Dante's crimson south wall and washed down two of the enormous tablets with which she'd so graciously supplied us. Thoughts of the coming high took the edge from the cheap beer, rendering it almost palatable. Jan smiled broadly and thanked us for our business by reaching beneath the table and giving mine and Jonny's members a rough squeeze. It was her way. We rose, the feeling of her eyes washing over our back sides an almost physically perceivable thing, and slid out the door. The night air smacked of possibility as we proceeded northward, back toward the den. And though we were starting late, our spirits were good. Acid is a prime time drug, which is to say that it needs be ingested by 8 p.m. Any later than this prescribed hour can prove, chronologically speaking, disastrous. Duration of effect is the primary reason one need observe the simple but paramount prime time rule. It is not uncommon to feel lingering traces of incapacitation 15 to 20 hours after administration of that sinister poison.

It was after midnight when the first whispers of expansion crept up my spinal cord, convinced my medulla to keep the heart and lungs running no matter what the cerebellum dictated, then advanced into my cerebrum where it wreaked havoc on thought and perception alike.

Pedal to the metal, Renault 18i station wagon humming like an overboosted sewing machine. Jonny, at my right, sat white knuckled, sweating. "You're gonna roll it man!" he shrieked as I cut homicidally in and out of traffic. My chemically twisted mind had arrived at the conclusion that I was Pharaoh, God on earth, son of Seth, Egyptian god of fear, loathing, hate, and war. The little, piece-of-French-shit car had been transformed. It was my royal chariot and I would maneuver it as I pleased.

Car full of kids coming up on the right. Mom and Dad were arguing up front. Dad stared ahead. By all indications, the family drive had gone bad. Pops was angry, fuming in fact. He hated his wife. I could smell the loathing. It radiated from him like death from a trodden cobra. Our eyes met. Pops took comfort in my empathy. Misery loves empathy. We were getting somewhere, he and I—connecting out in the void. Anger was his drug—pure and powerful, a perfectly clean, medically undetectable high.

"We're all going to die! Death feeds indiscriminately!" Jonny's renewed ranting snapped our connection. Fury, primal rage and unparalleled hatred washed across Dad's face as he was left, once again, alone with the woman and children.

"For Christsakes, you're gonna roll it! Humans are sharks, man, they eat their weak and dead. If we roll it, this crazy fucker alongside…" he stabbed a thumb toward Pops. "…is gonna yank our charred corpses from the wreckage and feed us to his brood. See how he's *looking* at us." Jonny's entreaty drowned in a wave of vomit that streamed out the window from his grimacing mouth and paralleled the Renault for a few feet before atomizing into an unattractive vapor that fouled the windshields of twenty following automobiles.

Mom, in the meantime, had redoubled her commentary on the manner in which she thought Pops should drive; namely, away from the erratically lurching, blue station wagon filled with dangerous, hallucinogenically wasted hippies, and into the safety of east side, upper middle class suburbia—preferably at top speed.

Jonny cleared his throat and resumed his paranoid soliloquy where he'd left off. "She's encouraging him. Look how flushed she is! Maternal instinct. The matriarch bitch wants her litter fed, man! She's giving him a recipe! I just know it. She's driving him into a feeding frenzy. Brisket of contemporary musician steamed over ruptured radiator. Turn back, man! We have to bail!"

Pops grimaced in disgust as Jonny filled the rushing air stream between the two vehicles with evil effluent a second time. The situation was getting out of hand. Acquiescing to what seemed my future attorney's sound rationale, I veered away from the shaken family with a savageness that threatened to roll the Renault right off of its non-sporting suspension. Further instances of vomiting ensued. Acid, as a rule, did not cause its taker to vomit. Gas and mild bloating weren't uncommon, but regurgitation was not on the usual list of physiological side effects.

"It was that fucking fish!" Jonny gasped between fits of retching. "That goddamn red tide, deep-fried whatever it was. Damn! What I wouldn't give for a good kabonosa or some of your mom's golabki."

These were Polish delicacies, the first being a kind of jerked sausage, the second a cabbage stuffed with meat, rice and a spicy tomato sauce. Though I wasn't particularly hungry at the moment, the thought of good, ethnically correct cuisine did spark my imagination. I tucked the idea away as I endeavored to traverse Mercer Island sans headlamps.

It was 4:00 a.m. Pacific standard time and deep tripping, acid ramblings abounded. "Tell me more about the food, Jonny. Talk to me about borsch and pierogie."

"Yha, man. Pierogie. Listen, Scottie…" Jonny uttered the first words of what we would both later acknowledge as a statement of sheer genius and historical significance. "Have you ever thought of how easy it would be to phone up your mom and get some of her old recipes? I mean, Christ, these people out here would lose their fucking minds over a plate of kapusta (sauerkraut with beef, mushrooms, and sausage) and your grandfather's fresh kielbasa (sausage) with a side of chrcan (homemade horseradish)."

He had me thinking.

Stressed to the Canines

A bit of the roadside darkness suddenly detached itself from the ambient gloom and drifted casually, out in front of the speeding Renault. Jonny's features contorted and his body convulsed in preparation for the unavoidable impact.

For my own part, I had seen the phantom shape from several hundred yards up road, but dismissed it as a tacky figment of my dangerously over-boosted imagination. If, after all, I had slowed or altered course for every chemically concocted specter I had seen over the years, chances were I would have since expired in a myriad of overturned, ditch-planted automobiles.

"Aw shit, Scottie," Jonny cursed.

The energy of the impact surged through the car's frame with sickening brutality, but it was the noise, the deep, resonant sound of flesh and bone careening off steel that startled me most.

"What in the fuck was it?" I demanded of Jonny as I brought the car to a shrieking stop in the shoulder.

"Jesus, Scottie," he panted, "I think it was a dog. I can't be sure, though. At the last second I saw what looked like eyes. You know, animal eyes filled with headlights. I think we *killed* it, too."

The concern in Jonny's voice was completely uncharacteristic. It made me nervous.

"I don't give a good goddamn if it was a group of night school-going first-graders crossing the fucking street," I raged. "What about me? What about my car? Why can't you show me a bit of that special reserve sympathy you've whipped up for this alleged, suicidal dog?"

"Sorry, man," Jonny muttered, embarrassed. "It's just that I got a little scared there. It's not every night we kill something—you heartless bastard."

The return of Jonny's innate hostility set my mind at ease. "Let's go find it," I huffed. "It couldn't have gotten far. We must have been going forty-five or fifty when we hit the unfortunate son of a bitch."

"And what happens when we find it?" Jonny asked with a bit of trepidation.

At first, the question struck me as little more than an interesting, hypothetical scenario. I never expected to actually find the animal, so sure was I that it had either dragged itself back into the darkness from which it had come, to contort away its agonizing last moments in seclusion, or that the impact itself had launched the beast so far into the surrounding gloom, that God himself couldn't possibly locate it.

A pathetic sound of feeble, canine whimpering intermixed with labored breathing brought Jonny and me to instant attention. Flinging open our respective car doors, we stood in the half-light of the Renault's headlights, straining our eyes against the secretive night.

"There!" Jonny spat, gesturing wildly toward the front bumper.

"What?" I demanded. "There's nothing there."

"Jesus, Scottie," Jonny sounded panicky. "Come around to my side. I don't know if I can handle this, man."

I stepped briskly around the front of the idling car and nearly wept for what I saw lying before me. Jutting from under the radiator intake, the battered head of a handsome, black Labrador Retriever lolled in apparent unconsciousness. I dropped to my knees beside the visible portion of the animal and, as I did so, its deep, almond-colored eyes fluttered open and regarded me with mild curiosity. Had I not known better, I would have sworn that look had in it both forgiveness for me and my questionable driving, as well as a taint of embarrassment on the part of the dog. It was as if the brute was saying…

Sorry, man. My fault.

"Don't talk," I instructed the animal. "We'll wade through this shit together. One way or another, you'll see the miserable sun rise."

"I know," Jonny agreed. "I appreciate your concern."

Jonny had assumed I was addressing him. His reaction did, of course, make perfect sense. Who in his right mind would pander to a dog's limited intellect by actually *talking* to it?

I looked away, trying to clear my head of what suddenly seemed a more treacherous high than I'd originally thought. Craning my neck painfully skyward, I surveyed a point of light I now know to be Venus and assured myself that my suspected communication with the dog had been completely one-sided. I maintained this posture until the pain in my neck and shoulders forced me to return my gaze to the mangled animal.

Are you finished, Sir? If so, I would greatly appreciate any assistance you might proffer me.

I reeled. The evil animal had invaded my sanity a second time and was somehow speaking to me. I wrenched my face from that of the unwholesome beast and frantically scanned the darkness for Jonny. After a moment, I discerned his silhouette pissing into a culvert some 10 feet from the scene of our crime against the local fauna.

"Jonny," I pleaded. "Do you hear anything?"

"Only my stomach, Scottie," he answered. "We really do need to stop by a Denny's and get a bite to eat. Is it dead yet?"

"No, it most certainly isn't dead yet, you morbid cocksucker," I chided. "Now get the fucking jack out of the car. We have to get this dog to a hospital before one of its major systems craps out."

"A hospital?" Jonny demanded incredulously. "Am I to understand that you intend to whisk that cadaver-in-waiting off to an otherwise sanitary hospital? Do you really think they're going to admit it? And what about the two of us? If

I may say so, you don't look so hot, certainly not well enough to calmly fill out hospital forms in the presence of a health care professional—a trained nurse who knows a thing or two about substance abuse and its symptoms."

He was right. There was no way in Hell we could pull it off. We were on our own.

I understand.

The dog's voice welled up in my ears.

All I ask is that you do your best. No hard feelings if it doesn't work out. By the way, I'm Bro.

The dog curled his great jowls into a remarkable facsimile of a smile while I clutched my temples in horrified disbelief. Could this really be happening? I forced myself into an approximation of calm and, without speaking, addressed the brute.

"Hello, Bro," I concentrated, "I'm Scottie Scirocco. The pissing bandit over there is Jonny S. I'm very sorry about all of this. You see, we, Jonny and I, are a bit twisted on drugs this evening. To that end, I need to know if this little chat we're enjoying is really transpiring, or if I need that hospital worse than you do."

Perfectly understandable, Scottie. Please take note. This 'chat', as you call it, is completely legitimate, one hundred percent on the up and up. You see, as much as you conceited, up-fuckish humans would like to think that you've got the sentience market cornered—you don't. It's best we leave it at that for the time being. I would very much like to dispense more information, but I seem to be bleeding to death just now.

Indeed, Bro's situation was worsening. "Jonny, where's that goddamn jack!" I shrieked, just as the awkward implement clattered to the ground beside me. "About time," I rebuked him.

"It's not like I didn't have to unload four hundred pounds of gear to get at it, you ungrateful prick," he countered.

Upon closer inspection, I beheld guitars, amplifiers, all manner of effect boards, and what appeared to be several miles of cable draped over and around the car. How could I not have noticed Jonny's diligent, not to mention exceedingly noisy, labors unless…

I turned, once again, to face the dog, who shot me a conspiratorial wink then grimaced in pain.

Menage á' Triage

I had argued hotly against involving Jan in the evening's madness, but Jonny's insistence and Bro's declining condition left me little choice but to acquiesce and point the Renault toward her eastside digs. It turned out to be a good call on Jonny's part.

We phoned Jan from a gas station five blocks from her home and filled her in on the sordid details. By the time we arrived, she had prepared the domestic equivalent of an inner city trauma unit around her dining room table. The autoclaves she used to sterilize her trade paraphernalia were arranged in a semi-circle on her kitchen counter, busily cooking the disease from an impressive array of vascular clamps (roach clips), surgical tubing (tourniquets), and suture needles (suture needles). A hardbound volume of *Gray's Anatomy*, which I doubted would be of any real value, sat at the ready.

Jonny and I bore the incoherent animal through Jan's front door with the delicacy of a pair of NFL running-backs en route to the opposing end zone.

"Over here, guys," she called from the dining room.

She spent the better part of the next 90 minutes hovering over and around the incapacitated dog. At times her actions implied confidence. The practiced way she guided needle after oozing needle into the beast's fur-obscured veins, for example, filled me with heady optimism. At other times, however, it was apparent she was free-forming. Jan's novice manipulation of a sub-dermal irrigator (a dime store squirt gun filled with distilled water), nearly proved disastrous. In her haste to cleanse the road rubble from Bro's tattered flesh, she inadvertently refilled the gun with rubbing alcohol instead of water. A cacophony of pitiable squealing exploded from the dog and Bro twisted in such a way that he very nearly fell from the table. Had such a calamity occurred, the tangle of I.V. tubes protruding from his freshly splinted limbs would have torn loose and that, as it is said, would have been that. The hasty addition of a Phenobarbital drip calmed the dog and brought the situation back to order. Jan regarded Jonny and I sheepishly. "Sorry, guys," she muttered.

"No need, Jan," I assured her. "We appreciate this more than you know."

Her ego appeased, Jan once again turned her full attention on the patient. Amazingly, none of Bro's vital organs seemed to have been displaced or ruptured in the collision. Aside from a number of fairly deep lacerations, which Jan sutured neatly, and a fractured pelvis, the dog had somehow escaped catastrophic injury.

Rinsing the thick, canine blood from her hands, Jan suggested we allow the beast to sleep a while before trying to rouse him. The ensuing hours passed in tense silence. Jonny yanked away at the joystick of Jan's archaic, Atari home video game system while I perused a stack of *High Times* magazines. Jan put on a pot of coffee and chain-smoked between periodic checks of the dog's vital signs. Only the deep and abiding friendship the three of us shared made the situation tolerable.

Jan snapped a pair of smelling salts beneath the dog's nose. Immediately, his nostrils dilated and he instinctively tried turning his head from the offensive stink.

"That's it, big boy," she encouraged, "Give mama a sign that she didn't fuck you up worse than you were when you got here."

Jesus Christ, Scottie, what the hell is that thing she's

waving under my nose. Do you realize how much more acute my sense of smell is than that of a human? Make her stop before I maul her.

I was horrified at the arrogant prick's ingratitude. "She just saved your worthless life, you indignant pig," I silently chided. "Now knock off that self-centered bullshit before I drag you out to the driveway and back over you just to make a point."

He seemed to accept the reason in what I was telling him. I was learning that Bro responded better to crass directness than he did to more socially accepted euphemism. The animal apparently found some perverse satisfaction in confrontation. I rather admired this about him. Judging by the placid contentment into which the dog sank, I concluded that the feeling was mutual. He liked me.

I found myself wondering where the developing, lunatic situation would lead as I watched Jonny and Jan share a triumphant embrace. They'd become oblivious to me, leaving me to steep—alone in the beast's affable presence.

Acquisition and Departure

Flash one year into the future: My and Jonny's heavy metal career had crashed and burned. Our lifestyle went with it. Six months later, in an act of ugly desperation, we sheared away our long hair. We were left a pair of ordinary, average, if not slightly twisted fellows surveying the remains of our rock and roll fantasy against the harsh backdrop of late twentieth century America. No expenditure of paper and ink could accurately relate the number of times Jonny's words, "Humans are sharks, man. They eat their weak...and their dead," sounded like the knelling of funeral bells in my mind as I went through the motions of one-entry level job after another.

It was intolerable. It had to stop. I saw to it that it did.

In September of 1990, Bro and I bid farewell to Jonny and Jan, trusting they would keep one another entertained, and set off for Mexico. My meager savings would go a long way there and the dry climate would ease the dog's arthritic agony...or so I rationalized.

Knowing the Renault wouldn't survive the arduous journey south, I dumped it for a song and applied the minimal proceeds to the purchase of a green Dodge van. Peculiar to the van and, in retrospect, the reason I purchased it instead of the cherry red Vega I'd had my eye on, was a bizarre and fascinating painting ornamenting one of the vehicle's interior walls.

Resplendent in natural tans and lifelike shades of pink, an anatomically ludicrous caricature of a donkey had been rendered just above the Dodge's rear, right side wheel well. To offset the beast's juvenile, comedic quality, the artist had (in what must have been an exhaust fume-induced delirium) appended to it a penis of positively enormous size and painful looking turgidity. Upon my discovery of the painting, the salesman showing me the van stammered out a protracted string of lame excuses and assured me that the "graffiti," as he called it, would be removed should I decide to purchase the vehicle. I forbade it and explained to him that any attempt on his or the dealership's part to remove, or in some way censor, the erotic masterpiece would result in my immediate departure from the lot. Money changed hands. It was obvious that the dealership was as glad to be rid of the automotive curiosity as I was to acquire it.

Six hours into our odyssey, Bro manifested an unnatural interest in the illustration.

Seventy miles north of Sacramento, he woke from a late morning nap and, unbuckling his seat belt, sauntered to the rear of the van where he sat, rapt in mute amazement, before the brazen painting.

Do you think it's possible? he inquired of me. *I mean, wouldn't the little shit be blacking out? How much spunk*

could the cardio-vascular system of such a small animal possibly have? Certainly not enough to meet the erectile demands of a prick that size. Just look at the thing for Christsakes. It's like something Upton Sinclair would have written about. How much longer until we're there? You drive like a nearsighted drug smuggler who's just noticed a cop easing up behind him. You really should consider giving me a little wheel time. I'm too old to fuck around. I'd get us there in style.

I was in no mood for the dog's pompous bullshit.

"Dog is a delicacy in Tijuana," I happily announced. "I was thinking; if I run out of cigarette money, I can always sell you to a hard-up cantina proprietor for at least fifteen dollars, American."

I was compelled to turn around when, after several seconds, I'd received no rebuttal to my brilliant quip. What I beheld compelled me to bellow in horrified revulsion.

Bro had assumed a pose similar to that of the painted burro and was regarding his own flaccid, rather uninspiring penis with obvious frustration.

Do you think if I went on a higher protein diet that things would be different, or do...

"You sick, fucked up psychopath!" I admonished him. "What kind of twisted role-playing lunacy is this? What's next? Am I going to wake up tonight to find you devouring chuck steaks in hopes of measuring up to a cartoon jackass with a superimposed dork? I thought you were smarter than that."

I knew I'd struck a nerve with the intelligence comment. Bro nurtures a preoccupation with the paranoid delusion that because he is a dog, people look down on his cognitive abilities.

Of course I'm smarter than that—you cruel pimp of a man. It's just that I'm so painfully hot, miserably bored, and ravenously hungry, I can't keep my thoughts straight. I'm afraid I'll lose my mind if we don't stop in the next town.

He had a point. It had been nearly ten hours since we'd left the chic sophistication of the Emerald City. The coffee had gotten progressively worse as we continued south and so had the climate. The soothing cool of Seattle's overcast skies had given way to Portland's partly cloudy atmospheric indecision and now, six hundred miles from home, the Northern California sun was beating both me and the dog into submission.

Thoughts of food, air conditioning and perhaps even a bit of sleep had been haunting me since we crossed the Oregon-California border. I hadn't mentioned it to the dog though. Notions of leisure, once planted in the stubborn animal's mind, were all but impossible to remove. It had been my plan to make it as far as San Francisco that first day. I knew if I could convince Bro to go along with my designs that we'd have a good start to our Mexican hiatus and the following day would entail less driving.

"Can you stand two more hours on the road if I let you listen to the Walkman?" I pensively asked him.

And what reward shall I have for my continued patience and good humor? he responded, all the while trying to tilt his ears forward—burro style.

"I'll get us a good hotel room in Frisco and tomorrow, since we'll have time to spare, we can go to the waterfront and play 'blind man and noble seeing-eye dog.' I know how much you love the attention you get when we do that tired routine. What do you say?"

What tape do you have in the Walkman?

He was buying into my plan.

"I have Uriah Heap in it right now, but there's some Alan Parson's Project around here somewhere."

That last one did the trick. The sappy son of a bitch was a sucker for dramatic instrumentals. He claimed they eased the pain in his joints. He spent the next 200 miles listening contentedly to The Alan Parson's Project's *Pyramid* album. My god had not, it seemed, forsaken me.

Art Is Where You Find It

Neither of the first two San Francisco hotels I tried permitted dogs on premises. Bro and I were forced to cross over into Oakland where finally, I was able to secure lodgings for us at a rather upscale affair called Jack London Square.

The "Square," as the locals call it, is a lonely outpost of culture and genuine civilization that stands in conspicuous contrast to the stark wilds of greater Oakland. The discriminating connoisseur can purchase crack cocaine at the square's front gate, then retire to its tranquil interior to enjoy his purchase with a seven dollar gin and tonic. It was, in a word, mine and Bro's kind of place.

We settled into our third floor room and, after a pair of long showers, phoned up the concierge for a dinner recommendation. She glibly suggested a neighboring fish house called Scotties. The name appealed to my sense of vanity and 15 minutes later, Bro and I found ourselves enjoying the air conditioned luxury of the restaurant's lobby.

Not surprisingly, the hostess flatly refused to seat us— yet another obtrusive "no animals" policy. I was ready for such a contingency, however, and produced from my coat pocket a compact disc copy of Iniquity's EP release. I waved the CD in the hostess's face, taking special care to emphasize the gleaming photograph of my own handsome face on the back cover. Leaning over her podium, I confided that I was "Elton Springsteen Simmons," internationally renowned rock icon and sometime frequenter of the Bay Area. The dog, I explained, was my food taster.

The good people at Warner Brothers—my record label—in recognizing my value to their company, had written a clause into my contract which clearly stipulated that any and all food I consumed outside the Warner Brother's cafeteria must first be tasted by a trained explosives dog.

One never knew when the envious savages at Atlantic or Polydor might stoop to assassination.

She glanced skeptically at me, searching my face for some hint of dishonesty. Finding none, she became visibly excited by the prospect of rubbing elbows with a genuine rock star, and hurriedly showed the dog and me to one of the restaurant's better tables.

"Art is where you make it," I beamed as the hostess scampered away to fetch liquor and ashtrays.

"What will you be dining on this fine evening?" I then inquired of my companion.

Swordfish, and a nice cognac for dessert, he answered without hesitation.

"Excellent choice," I observed. "Perhaps I'll have the same."

Rock stardom has its privileges. Both Elton Springsteen Simmons and his faithful taster enjoyed lavish meals and obscene amounts of spendy liquor that evening. Some time long after the barkeep sounded last call, Bro vomited up $50 or $60 worth of cognac. Blind with drink myself, I bellowed something about arsenic in the string beans, collected my dog, and stormed from the establishment in a masterfully feigned fit of indignation.

Paraffin and its Pitfalls

The San Francisco waterfront was alive with diversity the following morning. Individuals, compelled by mad muses to express themselves in wildly unorthodox ways, pushed the envelope of good taste to dizzying extremes.

Stunning drag queens pranced and cavorted along the Pier 33 boardwalk while Midwestern parents snapped pictures of their children clambering up a 10-foot, plastic replica of Bugs Bunny. Japanese tourists crowded harbor boats en route to Alcatraz Island, completely unaware of the teenage pickpockets who moved through their ranks with practiced ease, relieving them of wallets, cameras and other valuables. It was all too beautiful.

"Isn't America great?" I asked out loud.

Go fuck yourself. I hope each and every one of these people drops dead before noon, or, at the very least, is stricken mute.

The previous evening's overindulgence was taking its toll on the dog. The cognac had exacted a heavy toll on him during the night. I'd tried to warn him about the French poison, but he'd paid me little mind and went on swilling like a fish until he'd lost his guts.

I don't know how long I can hold out, he lamented. *The sun is cooking my eyes, and my tongue has a hard on. I need aspirin.*

I had no aspirin, but getting the dog out of the sun was easy enough. Two blocks north of Pier 33 stood an ominous, rather promising looking wax museum toward which I ushered the pitiable beast.

I paid the $8 cover and hurried Bro into the soothing darkness. The elderly museum attendant who collected my money glanced at the dog as if he was a duffel bag and went back to staring out his window. A man taking his dog to the wax museum apparently scored rather low on the San Francisco weirdness index.

It was fortunate that the museum's first exhibit, the British Royal Family, was situated around a corner and out of the doorman's line of sight. Retching uncontrollably, Bro staggered into the Queen Mother and vomited violently upon her taffeta gown. He was in worse shape than I'd originally thought.

Beg your pardon, Highness, he apologized, flecks of vomit spraying from his jowls. *Yes, that's better,* he conceded after a moment. *Let's cut through the bullshit and head straight on down to the chamber of horrors. I can't see any reason for us to stand here looking at the Duke of York when we could be down in the ruts with Jack the Ripper and Lizzy Borden.* He regarded me contemptuously. *Lead on then, you procrastinating coward.*

Removal of his aging carcass from the sun seemed to have done instant wonders for the dog's disposition. In the interest of avoiding a scene, I elected to humor the animal's deviant tastes and followed a series of signs to the "Medieval Dungeon," which turned out to be a rather silly affair remplete with black lights and a mechanical Frankenstein monster.

Yes, indeed, the dog's voice rang in my head like an activated smoke detector. *This is it, Sir. This is what living is all about. Who the fuck wants to look at normal, day-in and day-out crap when just a few yards away he can have release?*

Without further preamble, the dog left my side and sauntered over to a grotesque depiction of the Salem witch trials. He stared intently at the likeness of a young woman, her paraffin lips frozen in a silent shriek of frustration and horror, whose death loomed in the form of a black-hooded executioner setting ablaze an enormous bundle of kindling around her and the creosote-covered stake to which she was bound. Disinterested townspeople went about their daily business in the scene's background, oblivious to the heinous goings-on.

Of particular interest to the dog was the hoary figure of a shepherd that stood near the exhibit's rear, drawing water for his assembled sheep. It was one of these that Bro suddenly leapt upon with savage vigor, and, to my alarm, began to rape, all the while braying like an ass.

Take it, you stoic bastard, he snarled. *I'll pump you till your glass eyes fall out. Don't think I won't. I'll saw away at you backside until your haunches melt and this musty pelt of yours catches fire. Now show me some enthusiasm.*

The situation was completely out of hand. I jumped the

exhibit's velvet ropes and seized the mad animal by his tail, effectively disconnecting him from his inanimate playmate. I was beyond embarrassment and well on my way to anger.

"Why me?" I wondered. "Have I really led such a worthless life that I actually deserve this insanity, or is this the high karmic price of vehicular assault?"

Museum security had witnessed the entire shameful spectacle on closed circuit television and we were thrown from the building like common vandals. In retrospect, this was fortunate. Had I been made to pay for the damage my inept and socially irresponsible companion had wrought on the museum's collection, I would likely still be in debtor's prison.

We collected ourselves from the sidewalk and limped back to the green Dodge from which Bro had derived too much inspiration. It was time to get out of San Francisco.

The Government Made Me Do It

One hundred ten m.p.h. with another inch to go before the accelerator pedal hit the floor; the van's engine shrieked as if horrified as I urged the Mopar beastie through the southern California night. Flirting with death, I removed my eyes from the weather-beaten ribbon of highway and chanced a glance at the dog. To my right, Bro stood in the passenger seat, his head out the window, trailing snot and slobber down the vehicle's flanks. The scene suddenly reminded me of the night he and I had first crossed paths. Without thinking, I reached over and stroked his glossy black coat.

"Good boy," I crooned.

At once, his body stiffened. Pulling his mucous-streaked head back into the van, he regarded me with a disdainful look.

How dare you patronize me? he fumed, indignant. *You, Sir, are a condescending prick.*

I was appalled. My sincere intention had been to show the ungrateful brute a moment's affection and this is how he repaid me.

I was about to loose the verbal onslaught of my young life when, with a surprising and disturbingly human smile, the dog sauntered into my lap, licked my face, and lay his head out my window for what turned out to be an awkward but not altogether disagreeable roll of the odometer. Life seemed particularly sweet in that moment. The dog slept in my lap until my legs went completely numb and I began to doubt my continuing ability to safely drive. I roused him ten miles from the Mexican border.

"Bro, time to get up, old man," I urged. "My legs are asleep. If you don't get off of them I'm not going to be able to hit the brakes at Customs."

It sounds silly, but at the time it was a legitimate concern. For the last hour I had been forced to visually check my right foot to make sure it hadn't fallen from the accelerator—toward the brake pedal, and a hideous roll over accident. With less complaining than I'd expected, the dog rose, favored me with one of his long, halitosis-tainted yawns, and slunk off to the back of the van.

Fifteen minutes later I'd eased the dusty Dodge alongside a U.S. Customs Service booth, and was waiting anxiously for one of the three, bleary-looking agents to make his way over to us. I didn't have to wait long.

The nameplate opposite the man's badge identified him as Customs agent "Hicks," and he looked every bit the name. Wiry hair jutted out from beneath his government issue ball cap, forming a crazed horizontal halo around his red, acne-scarred face. Beads of sour-smelling sweat clung to his nose and ears. I realized in that unattractive moment that I'd never before seen a man's ears sweat. I was fascinated. Agent Hicks had about him a look common to veteran government employees—irritated boredom. I immediately pegged him a dangerous man, sure to be a hindrance to our prospective Mexican holiday. I waited patiently as Agent Hicks cross-checked the van's license plate against what must have been a list of stolen vehicles. Satisfied with the results of his search, he urged his considerable bulk upright and came around to my unrolled window.

"Mind showin' me yer driver's license and registration?" he began, sweat flecking from his lips and collecting in drops on his capacious earlobes.

"No, sir, not at all," I obligingly answered, handing him the bits of paper.

Hicks took a disquietingly long time comparing my face to that depicted on the driver's license. He asked me to open the hood so he could cross-check the vehicle identification number listed on the registration against the engine stamp. Once again, I did as he asked. It was becoming increasingly obvious that Hicks either disliked hippies or was bucking for a promotion. Probably the former, given the general impression of sloth he radiated.

"Do you have anything to declare, Mister Scirocco?" (he pronounced it see'-ru-ko).

The question struck me as rather strange.

"No sir, I don't," I politely answered. "And besides, wouldn't I normally declare something on my way back into the country?"

Big mistake. Hicks flushed crimson as anger and blood poured into his unattractive face.

"Are you questioning an officer of the United States Customs Service, you little shit?" he spat.

I had to back down, pronto.

"No sir, not at all, it's just that…"

I felt Bro's hot breath on my right cheek and turned to give the dog a quick look of warning. We didn't need more trouble than we already had.

The sudden appearance of a large, irritable-looking ani-

mal startled Hicks and he took a few tentative steps backward. He regained his composure, however, and marched
back to my window, his hand resting on his service revolver.
He was just beginning to say something when the dog's
voice crackled to life.

These are not the droids you are looking for.

"What?" I stammered.

They can go about their business.

I regarded the dog, wide-eyed, and whispered, "What in
God's name are you talking about, you crazy bastard."

Hicks seized me by the collar and hauled my head
through the window, out into the oppressive heat and the
even more disagreeable reek of his breath and stained uniform.

"I'll tell you what in God's name I'm talking about, you
punk faggot," he hissed. "I'm talking about transporting
contraband livestock over a national border. That's a crime,
boy, punishable by six months in federal prison." Hicks
paused, an ugly smile turning the edges of his ugly mouth.
"I can't tell you how good it's gonna feel to haul your ass
in," he concluded in a vulgar drawl.

"Livestock?" I implored, "That's not livestock. That's
my dog—my dog, for the christsake."

A look of concern flashed across Hicks' face. With
trembling hands, he pulled a pair of smudged bifocals from
his pants pocket, and eased them on.

"I'll be damned," he stated matter of factly. "I'm sorry,
son. This isn't the livestock we're looking for. You can go
about your business."

I engaged the transmission and accelerated into Mexico,
periodically regarding the once-again sleeping dog with
more than a little concern.

Experimental Dining

W e were racing through the Mexican night, about 50 miles south of Tijuana, when I beheld a suspicious glow illuminating the gentle crest of an upcoming rise in the highway. I was just beginning to strain my eyes in earnest against the darkness, trying to identify the source of the strange light, when the dog emerged from the inky cabin behind me.

Taco joint ahead, he grumbled, hauling himself into the passenger seat.

I was amazed.

"You can see that far?" I marveled.

No, but I've been smelling it for ten minutes. We should stop. I'm seldom wrong about food, and these tacos smell top notch—authentic shit, man.

We crested the hill and there, just as Bro had foretold, stood an honest-to-God, mom and pop, Mexican taco emporium. The facade, intended to emulate the gaudy, white tile exterior of a '50s American drive-in, succeeded only in conveying squalor and potential food poisoning. A hand-painted sign that read "Taco Temple" stood just outside the establishment's mottled screen door and rotated merrily on what appeared to be the chopped, blue metal flake legs of an anachronistic backyard swing set.

Wonderful, I thought, *American tackiness permeates all things, perverts all cultures.* "Let's just keep going, and find a grocery store. I'll pick up some sausage and later tonight we can build a fire and roast weenies."

The dog turned and looked at me as if I had been reading from the Koran in Hebrew.

Are you mad, Sir? Why would I possibly stoop to eating charred, day-old sausage, when I can enjoy bona fide rain forest beef and goat cheese, layered in a hand-mashed tortilla? To Hell with you and your asinine grocery store.

I reluctantly urged the van into Taco Temple's parking lot, all the while wondering what kind of havoc bad Mexican food would wreak on the dog's digestive system.

"Taco Temple" was a misnomer. The restaurant's interior raised serious questions as to what kind of temple the place really was and in whose honor it had been erected. Grease that gave every impression of being decades old had solidified on every horizontal surface in the dining room. It horrified me to think of what the kitchen may have looked like. Even though I saw no roaches, I felt them—billions of compound eyes moving over me and countless mouth parts articulating in anticipation of my first, errant crumb.

The locals, however (judging by the throng of patrons packed into the dingy place) didn't share my reservations. Squealing children, dispatched by their parents to fetch hot sauce, moved unnoticed between knots of bandito-looking truckers who huddled around stand-up circular tables exchanging road yarns. Against the back wall a dilapidated, red vinyl booth facilitated a young couple's amorous groping while at the bar, matronly señoritas tried in vain to avert their greedy eyes from the tangled knot of limbs into which the lovers were steadily metamorphosing. Rhythms of consonants flowed together, coalesced in the air around us, blended into the rich strains of conversational Spanish that lent the third world social landscape a cosmopolitan flair. I waxed self-conscious suddenly, realizing the dog and I were the only gringos in the place. My epiphany of ethnicity, my fleeting moment of fear, failed to go unnoticed. A trio of what appeared to be Mexican Hell's Angels, their heavy leather and denim uniforms ridiculous against the desert panorama floating in the window behind the booth they occupied, came to predatory attention as the chemical signature of my trepidation wafted into the air. The sensation of their attention was immediate, and extremely disconcerting. Not one of them moved. Only a rapid succession of exchanged glances among them and quickening of their unintelligible conversation evinced the subtle shift in the mob's mentality toward the sinister. The change in their mannerisms filled me with an uneasiness reminiscent of my earliest drug paranoias and caused my bowels to churn.

The dog, who simply didn't dabble in social posturing, seated himself in a booth opposite the young lovers. I followed him, doing my best to remain cool under the weight of the bikers' stares.

The restaurant's menu was surprisingly diverse. Hunger flared, dull and aching in the hollow of my ribs, and began to undermine the apprehension fostered in me by the neighboring ruffians.

What's 'gross campee-oh'? Bro inquired, perusing the menu from over my shoulder.

"That's *eros compollo*, you idiot," I chided him, "It's sautéed chicken and mushrooms served over Spanish rice— good stuff."

Excellent, he crooned, *I'll have that.*

I had been leaning toward the pork flautas until the dog decided on *eros compollo*. Acquiescing to his good taste, I elected to have the same. Placing the menu back into its stand behind the napkin caddie, I raised my eyes, thinking to summon the establishment's lone waitress, only to find myself staring into the six, muddy brown eyes of the three Mexican bikers.

The smallest flashed a hideous, broken-toothed smile at me and, in horribly broken English, began;

"You, I think, are not from here, eh?"

Assuring myself there *was* a way out of that ugly mess that didn't involve an overnight stay in a Mexican hospital, I cleared my throat, smiled, and rolled the bones.

"Why no, I'm not," I stammered. "I'm from the U.S.— Seattle, to be specific."

All three ruffians stood their ground and smiled the detached smiles particular to the criminally insane. They apparently understood little English.

As if sent by God, the diminutive waitress, a woman of perhaps 80 years and not many more pounds, wedged herself between me and the bikers and asked whether I was ready to order.

Thoughts of food I might have been entertaining had vanished with the arrival of the criminals three at my table. I was about to send the old waitress away when it occurred to me her presence played into my favor. The bikers, I reasoned, would be less likely to rough me up in the presence of a lady—especially one who could have been any of their grandmothers.

"Dos eros compollo, por favor," I intoned in my best Spanish.

"Gracias, Señor," she nodded before pushing her way back through the bikers as if they were a group of potted palms.

"Yours are big, and many children are in the spelling bee," the talkative, little biker proudly announced.

What was he saying, I wondered. Was he mad? Would he follow up his unintelligible verbalization with an equally senseless double murder of American tourists?

Smile at him, you dim son of a bitch, the dog hissed, *He's trying to show off for you.*

It seemed far-fetched, but having no theories of my own, I heeded Bro's advice and favored the boorish little man with a patronizing smile. This seemed to gratify him tremendously and he took, once again, to his tongue.

"Flipper, Reagan, and many spoonfuls of under the newspaper," he blurted.

I smiled again despite my overwhelming urge to vomit at the man's unspeakably terrible breath.

The three bikers roared laughter and squeezed their collective bulk into the booth with me and Bro. The linguist offered me a cigarette, which I gladly accepted. We smoked, the bikers laughing moronically between long drags of what was clearly *not* a Marlboro, until the two plates of food arrived. I felt guilty eating in front of our new friends and offered the lads a bit of my own dinner, knowing full well the dog would not do likewise. Silence descended on the table like plague. Like monks before the Virgin, the bikers removed their leather caps and bowed their oily heads in thanks. In offering them my food, I had apparently done them a great honor. So great in fact, that tears appeared and began streaming down their sun baked faces.

"Guys, it's really no big deal. Just take what you want. Christ, it's only chicken," I rationalized, trying to downplay my gesture.

Offer them the van, stupid, the crass animal interjected, *They might make you El Presidente.*

"Can it, you heartless fuck," I hissed under my breath, "Can't you see these men are genuinely touched?"

From the edge of the restaurant's counter, the old waitress had witnessed the strange goings-on. Wiping her hands on the tatter of apron girding her midsection, she approached with the quiet confidence of a nurse coming to ease a terminal patient's suffering.

"Senor," she addressed me. "These men are gypsies. I know their kind well. Their lives consist of traveling north, to Tijuana, and begging pocket change from Americans come down from California to spend their paychecks on liquor and two-dollar whores. If they are successful, these gypsies might make twenty or thirty dollars, then come here for a bite to eat." She eyed the bikers, the emotion behind her dark-eyed gaze unreadable. "These men were not successful. That is why they so deeply appreciate your generosity."

The dog exploded.

Now you've done it, you short-sighted pansy, he snarled at me. *You've done the equivalent of feeding bipedal, Mexican kittens. Do you realize we're probably stuck with these failed beggars for life? Do you, dickhead, take these three underachieving panhandlers to be your lawful, wed-*

ded, wives—to have and to hold, to honor and post bail for, in sickness and in sickness, till Immigration and Naturalization do you part?

He was right. I saw it in the ruffians' eyes. I was their hero—and their meal ticket. In a word, I was fucked. The resolution of this potentially explosive situation was going to require extreme diplomacy. I needed time to think. Regarding the waitress, who still stood at the end of our table, I asked her to explain to my new friends that I would be on my way in a moment, and hoped they would accept a round of meals on me before I left. She conveyed the message, and to my deep and abiding horror, the men declined.

"Señor," she began, tactfully. "The *hombres* wish to remain in your employ."

"My employ?" I marveled.

"*Si,*" she confirmed. "They wish to accompany you on your travels, and render what assistance they can, in payment for your kindness. Gypsies are like that; it is their way."

So with that the Mexican Biker Gypsies joined Bro and me on what was fast becoming a memorable sailing into strange, strange waters.

Their names were Juan, Luis, and Pedro—and they were brothers. It was upon the elder, Juan's, recommendation that, 20 miles south of Taco Temple, we left the dusty two-lane highway and pointed the van out into the open desert.

I was able to divine by Juan's hand signals, and miserable English, that peace could be found in the desert night, peace and the agave cactus.

The agave is a specimen of flowering, desert flora from which tequila and mescal are distilled. More importantly, mescaline, the mild hallucinogenic drug, is also derived from the useful agave. I thought the latter a fortunate tidbit insomuch as the last day's events had rekindled my appetite for recreational pharmaceuticals. If I had to risk my life driving into the nocturnal wilds of the Mexican desert, I might as well do so in the names of social irresponsibility and drug abuse.

The headlights that had guided thin trickles of traffic over the lonely stretch of sun-bleached highway upon which we'd been traveling, faded into the darkness. Moonlit desert, lovely as it was hostile, yawned to the violet-black horizon on all sides of the speeding green Dodge. To my right, Juan sat gesturing out the window toward an outcropping of rock some miles in the distance.

"*Paraiso*," he smiled, and nodded enthusiastically.

"*Paraiso*," I now know, is the Spanish word for *paradise*. I wondered what Juan was getting at.

Twenty minutes later, leaning against the van's blisteringly hot hood with a bottle of home-distilled mescal in one hand and a joint, fatter than any I'd seen Stateside, smoldering in the other, I returned Juan's smile.

The Mexican Biker Gypsy Brothers had built their hideout wisely and well. Taking advantage of the secluded, desert rock formation, they had erected upon its ramparts a crude but well-fortified and reasonably comfortable fortress against the outside world. Luis and Pedro had leapt from the van before its old tires came to a crunching stop on the pebbly earth, and disappeared into the pitch black of a sheet metal shanty thrown up at west end of their compound. They'd emerged a few moments later carrying the case of mescal from which my bottle had come, along with a cigar box filled with doobies and a small leather pouch that contained a few ounces of dehydrated vegetation.

"*Bueno, bueno*," Juan exclaimed, patting his brothers on the back as they passed.

Luis and Pedro went quickly and quietly about the business of building a fire from dry wood taken from beneath an overturned oil drum. I watched the proceedings from against the van and was impressed by the orderly, indeed, military precision with which the men went about their work. Glancing back into the van's open side door, I noticed

Bro had removed himself from the sleeping bag in which he'd been holed up since we arrived at the biker's fortress. Not so much as the animal's musty scent (an aroma that conjured images of dry leaves laced with olive oil) remained to evince his recent occupancy.

"Probably gone off to take a refreshing piss," I surmised, and went back to watching our hosts make their preparations for whatever strange ritual they had planned to fill the long hours ahead.

I was surprised, upon returning my attention to the milling bikers, to see an inviting fire roaring where, moments ago, only chill and gloom had lingered.

The brothers arranged themselves around the warming glow, apparently making ready to do away with large volumes of tequila. It was Pedro, the small, talkative one, who motioned me to join them. I happily agreed and, crossing the growing gulf of darkness separating us, settled in amongst my benefactors.

We sat, drinking and smoking, for hours on end. I was amazed at how well the four of us were able to communicate in the absence of a common language. Juan began to tell what I assumed were jokes, and though I remained completely unable to understand the literal meaning of his words, the uproarious reactions of his brothers (not to mention the influence of the two bottles of mescal I'd downed) were enough to start me laughing along with them.

Socially speaking, things were going well. So well in fact that Juan deemed it time to move on to more exciting recreational options.

The leather pouch Luis and Pedro had brought from the shanty was, as I suspected, filled with dried agave. Juan secured my attention and, by example, demonstrated the correct technique for first re-hydrating the stuff by soaking it in a cup of mescal, then packing it, like tobacco, between the lower lip and gums. I watched intently as he and then his brothers performed the ritual.

When my turn came, I extracted a pinch, about the size of a parsley garnish, from the pouch and immersed it in a cup of mescal drawn from my bottle. Juan smiled approvingly as I packed my lip full of the horrid tasting vegetation.

Nothing; I felt no perceptible change in myself. The air tasted the same. The ground was down and the sky up. The stars seemed to remain in place. No change. Disappointed, I turned to Juan and motioned for more mescal.

"Sure, man," he replied, "But you should really pace yourself."

"Don't worry about me, *Patron*," I smugly replied. "I've been doing this a long time, and…"

The words dried up in my throat. Juan had spoken English—good English. I turned to Pedro, and the shy Luis.

"Can you two understand me?" I stammered.

Not surprisingly, it was Pedro who spoke up.

"Oh sure, man. We're down with you, Yankee man from Seattle. In fact, I'd like to take this opportunity, since Juan is an ill-mannered pig and hasn't properly done so, to thank you for sharing your eats back at the Taco Temple. We have tons of liquor and smoke stashed away here, but food is a problem. We've tried storing it in the past, but that's never worked. What the lizards don't eat spoils and the buzzards eat that. We've shown up here for overnight parties and, finding no food remaining, been forced to set traps for gila monsters and horned toads. One time, Luis here got himself so strung out on mescal and ditch weed that he made a fishing pole out of an old tire iron and some bailing wire. He spent half the night fishing off the west wall, behind the shack. On more than one occasion that evening, he began screaming that he had a bite and for one of us to bring a net. Juan finally had to hit him in the head with a burning log and drag him into the shack to sleep it off. Isn't that right, Luis?"

We both turned to face Luis, who had remained characteristically quiet and expressionless throughout Pedro's discourse.

"Isn't that right, Luis?" Pedro repeated.

"Christ, but I've fucked a ton of em!" Luis shrieked, without warning. "Who can count anymore?"

Pedro and I exchanged worried glances. It seemed no one was home at Luis's. Our eyes moved back to him. No sooner had we fixed Luis in our combined gaze than he resumed his incensed monologue.

"Dozens of em, boys. And all of them beautiful…well, most of them anyway. Do you remember that first one, Pedro? She was a red-haired farm girl who lived down the street from grandmother. I was just a kid at the time, maybe eleven or twelve years old. She was sixteen or seventeen and used to have her way with me in her old man's barn. I can still remember the sweet smell of fresh hay in the loft. She and I would roll around in it, kissing and groping one another, neither of us sure what to do beyond that point. We'd figured it out by summer's end, though. It was in her parents' tacky, light blue bedroom. The windows were open and a light breeze was blowing in, moving the drapes like dresses around listless women. I recall being very nervous about the fact that you and Juan were just outside, playing baseball with her brother and sister. We didn't have any rubbers—hell, we didn't think we would actually end up fucking—so I hiked my pants back up and hopped to the kitchen for a plastic sandwich bag. It was the best idea I could come up with at the time. Stumbling back to her parent's room, I found her lying naked. It was the loveliest thing I'd ever seen. She giggled a bit as I bagged my cock. Her giggles subsided when I mounted her, however.

"I'm proud to say, lads, that my first orgasm was with a real live girl. No shoddy wet dream or humiliating, accidental jerk-off for me. No sir. The fact that my dork never made it into her that first try is incidental. I hovered above her, you see, wrestling with the enormity of what we were about to do. Unversed in the ways of physical love, I made the mistake of chancing a glance down, between her legs and, POW! That was all it took.

"I'm telling you, Pedro, I thought I was dying. All those years of Catholic school came rushing up on me. I was sure the overwhelming sensation welling up from between my legs was the hand of God Almighty striking me down for my flagrant sinning. It felt as if my cock was pressurizing to the bursting point. The feeling started low in my gut and, before I knew it, had spread like a chemical burn, up my spine and into my lustful brain. 'This is it,' I thought. 'Luis is punching out, courtesy of a vengeful God.' But I didn't die. Instead, the pressure broke in wave after wave of blessed relief. It didn't take me long to figure out what had happened.

"It dawned on me, suddenly, that I had become so absorbed in my own bodily functions that I had completely forgotten about my partner. I looked up into her eyes and, instead of the disappointment I'd expected, found relief. She had apparently been mortified of losing her virginity to a sandwich-bagged cock. We kissed and later that afternoon, in a concession to her reservations, I fucked her in the ass.

"We went on like that, sodomy after sordid sodomy, for the remainder of the summer. Within a week of that first, clumsy fumbling, she had grown remarkably fond of anal sex and began insisting that I visit her each and every day after school for a bit of the old ass mastering. Being twelve years old and incurably horny, I was more than happy to oblige."

Pedro and I had begun to unconsciously distance ourselves from the delusional Luis.

"She was a firecracker, she was," he resumed. "But you boys know what? As spunky as that little country girl was, she was nothing compared to my first town girl."

Both Pedro and I groaned at the prospect of yet another, mescaline fueled story. Undaunted by our obvious lack of enthusiasm, Luis went glibly on.

"Her name was Emily and she remains, to this day, the only girl I have ever loved."

Luis looked down at his shoes, kicked a stone, and sat back down. Pedro and I were at a loss. We exchanged an uneasy glance and resolved to lose ourselves in the comforting depths of our mescal bottles. A moments later, Pedro addressed his rambling brother.

"So what about this town girl, Luis. Was she a good randy fuck as well?"

Luis sprang to his feet like a startled bush pig, pulled an evil-looking switchblade from his Levi's, and turned on Pedro.

"You're talking about the woman I love, you ruthless fuck. *Vete al carajo* (kiss my ass)."

"Hey, I didn't mean anything by it," Pedro backpedaled. "I was just trying to be polite, you know, act like I was interested in what you were saying."

"Oh," Luis mouthed, "I understand. Sorry, my brother."

The two men embraced and the incident was forgotten.

"How about you, man?" Pedro turned to me and casually inquired. "You ever do any good dog-fucking?"

I smiled uncomfortably and was about to politely sidestep the issue when I noticed that it was Bro, not me, to whom Pedro was speaking. Relief washed over me. I hadn't really wanted to answer the question. Bro, on the other hand, was his usual matter of fact self.

Why yes, Pedro, I have, in fact, done more than my fair share of dog-fucking.

I couldn't believe it. The dog was communicating with someone other than me. I felt a sharp pang of jealously race up my throat.

The voice of experience hummed to life in my head.

It's the drug, Scottie. Look again, it urged.

I did, and to my relief, the dog was sleeping soundly in the shadows just beyond the firelight. This fleeting hallucinatory episode raised a number of warning flags in my dis-

integrating mind. Who exactly had Pedro been talking to?
And why was the granite flat upon which we were standing,
randomly changing size and consistency.

"Guys," I ventured. "I think I've had enough. I'm going
to turn in now. Goodnight."

Their goodnight's sounded strange; disjointed and vulgar. They had also begun reverting back to Spanish. I was
able to make out only a few of their words.

"Yankee man from Seattle," they called, "Have you ever
done any good dog-fucking?"

I strained my eyes against the alcohol, the darkness, and
the drug, and was barely able to make out the dancing
images of the Mexican Biker Gypsy Brothers against the
backdrop of bright bonfire. To my horror, they all appeared
to be fucking wax sheep.

Juan had torn the head from his woolly concubine and
was passionately kissing its cold, unresponsive lips. Pedro
seemed to admire his brother's sense of romanticism, but
lacked his finesse insomuch as instead of venerating the
head he'd torn off his sheep with kisses, he licked the eyes
then threw it into the fire where it melted to nothing. I recognized Luis a few feet from his impassioned brothers. He
knelt humbly before his sheep and proposed marriage.

Bro rose from the sand girding the mad spectacle and
made his way toward me. He stopped five or six feet short
of my outstretched hand and began to bray.

One-Eighty

I woke the next morning to find no sign of the Mexican
Biker Brothers. The evidence of the strange and
debaucherous night past abounded, but as for Juan,
Luis, and Pedro—they were gone. Only Bro remained, a
fact for which I was grateful. He watched me from the van's

open rear door with mild interest as I rose from my place beside the fire's smoldering remnants and vomited on myself. Struggling mightily, I made my way across the insanely hot and bright sand, toward the van and the shade it promised. When I'd drawn close enough for Bro to address me in civilized conversational tones, he yawned a fantastic, tongue curling yawn and began—

Just before sunrise, they stood up, shook the sand from themselves, pissed out the fire, more or less, and disappeared down the road on foot. Luis was good enough to turn you on your side in case your vomitous episode had occurred before you woke.

"Very noble of him," I wheezed.

Scottie...

"Yeah, Bro."

Let's go home, man. This dry climate is succeeding only in making me thirsty, my arthritis doesn't feel any better and I could really use a good cup of coffee.

The very notion of good coffee was motivation enough to make me swallow my pride and admit to the dog that my entire Mexican sabbatical idea had been short-sighted and stupid. He agreed enthusiastically.

I had an additional retch for good measure, then climbed into the driver's seat. We would take our time getting home. I figured my savings could withstand American restaurant and hotel rates for about a year.

By the time we returned to Seattle, Jonny had taken a revolting position as a hunter-seeker attorney at a collection agency and had found a way to keep his prolific appetite for top shelf pharmaceuticals discreetly under wraps. He and I picked up where we'd left off. Weekends we would patronize pubs and dance clubs. The world was disintegrating around us, though. The only constant seemed to be Jan. She had grown both physically and financially. It was rumored that she left her crimson couch in Dante's front dining room only for physiological reasons—which was more indicative

DOC SOLOMMEN

of sound business sense than a weak bladder. A new generation of clientele had emerged to replace has-beens the likes of Scottie Scirocco and Jonny S. These kids redefined hardcore. Herb was nothing—an hors de'oeuvre for the slick, designer chemicals upon whose tertiary structures was laid the unpredictable foundation of a new, decidedly riskier drug culture.

Ecstasy, Crack, Crank, Crystal Meth—even the names seemed brutal and indiscriminate. But what profit margins! With few exceptions, the hallmark of these new agents was the relative brevity of their discernable effects. Ten dollars worth of crack was good for maybe a 30-minute ride. After that, it was back to Jan for another dime ticket to transient Nirvana.

She was tired, though. Tired of the covert lifestyle her profession demanded, and old enough to have come to the realization that money wasn't everything and that work, old fashioned, dick in the dirt work, brought with it a sense of pride that all her amassed fortune could not afford her.

August, 1990: Jonny and I were deep into the late-night craziness, trying to recapture a past relegated to dim memory and rationalizations of not having known better. The blood flowing through our alcohol systems was hot that night as Jonny and I swaggered into Dante's foyer. And though we thought ourselves brave, neither of us was prepared for what awaited us behind the bar's heavy, wood plank door. The world *had* moved on. Accelerated away, in fact. Judas Priest 45s had been replaced in Dante's juke box by CD singles of something called Faster Pussycat. Dante's decor remained unchanged in theme but diminished, indeed crippled in intensity. Satan had apparently slipped from popularity—riding out of town with Judas Priest as it were. Where once his evil countenance leered in strikingly lifelike papier-mâché effigy, there remained only a huge, inflatable bottle of Budweiser. The Prince of Darkness, his majesty doused in Saint Louis pilsner, had been relegated to a back corner where he served as a pool cue rack. A half-dozen warped billiard sticks jutted from his eyes and a pair of triangles suspended from his once magnificent but now largely cracked and peeling ears. All and all, a very unsettling scene—especially to a pair of the Devil's dangerously intoxicated former admirers.

A shrill voice from across the room, "Well I'll be damned!" Jan had spotted us, and to the despair and desperation of her clients, was suspending business and rising from her *office* to offer warm salutations to a couple of, what the loitering kids must have perceived as, unreconcilably geeky businessman types. Jan dropped her hands to her sides and made a series of grasping motions as she approached us. For a rancid moment I actually thought she was going to inspect our wares. Her pantomime groping ceased at the last moment, however, and Jan's fleshy arms darted out, encircling our necks in a prolonged group hug.

"Fuck me dead, it's great to see you two," she beamed.

Exchanged pleasantries, embarrassing reminiscence, and awkward silence finally gave way to sincere conversation. Jan dismissed her customers, asking them to return in 30 minutes and assuring them she would not leave with Jonny and Me.

"Jan," Jonny began when the last of her lethargic clientele had loped off like a bitter sloth. "We have a proposition for you." I noted with satisfaction the subtle change in his mannerisms that evinced Jonny's shift into attorney mode.

"Thought you'd never ask, Jon," she fired back. "Just yourself, or both of you at once? You do know Leon's and my divorce is final. We maintain a strictly professional relationship. You know that, don't you?"

"Tempting as that may sound, Jan, this is a business, as in cash dollars business, proposition," Jonny persisted.

"Ah! Almost as good. Go ahead."

And so it began. Jonny delved into the plan he had conceived years ago; a plan involving my mother's and grandmother's ethnic dishes and the formulation of a menu the likes of which Seattle had never seen, a plan based on bold tastes and exotic ingredients, cuisine that would appeal to an upscale, gourmet crowd that was turning a disenchanted cold shoulder toward the once hip Mediterranean establishments that loosely delineated the last wave of dining innovation to sweep the Jet city. He explained how with his vision, my resources and, most importantly, Jan's financial backing, we three could spawn the most riotously successful eatery since The Canlis.

To our surprise and, quite frankly, disbelief, Jan immediately agreed to our initial request for $150,000 in start up capital. By evening's end, she had proclaimed herself far too financially potent to deal in fractions and upped the ante to a cool 200 grand.

It was another one of Jonny's strokes of sheer marketing genius which led us to christen the first restaurant Scirocco Taco.

"Its not fucking Mexican food, Jon," I would protest in those early days.

"Look, Scottie," he'd counter. "People are going to love the food. They won't realize that, though, until they're coerced into trying it. I mean...shit, I wouldn't eat a kiszka if I knew what it was. Why, it's a fucking barley and blood sausage junked up on sage and pepper. It looks revolting. We need to get people in the door. Just get them in the goddamn door. See my point? Everyone likes Mexican food. Even if they're not crazy about it, it at least strikes them as normal. We'll call the place Scirocco Taco, make the building look like the Alamo or some such ridiculous thing, and pipe in bad, AM Mariachi music. People come in, peruse the menu, chalk their unfamiliarity with the fare up to their own shoddy comprehension of the Spanish language, then order to save face in front of the Guadalajaran wait staff we're going to hire. Hell, there's nothing more embarrassing than getting up and leaving a restaurant once you've endured the baleful scrutiny of an epicurean Mexican waiter. People will *have* to try the food."

Thirteen months later, a structure resembling a Spanish mission was erected on the corner of California and Fauntleroy in West Seattle. In a hard-won concession to my sense of ethics, a Polish flag was flown proudly above the adobe ramparts—a bizarre spectacle by any stretch of the imagination. The time of reckoning descended upon us. We'd run our idea up the proverbial flag pole and waited tensely to see who would salute it.

As it turns out, the salute was universal. Scirocco Taco was an overnight hit. Food critics raved. The public swooned. Seven nights a week the dining room was booked solid with 10 hours of firm reservations. Standing room only was the norm for the bar. We accepted every credit card known to man and after a month, we were sure we'd billed every credit card held by man. Two years later, a subsidiary restaurant, Cassa Kielbasa, opened in Bellevue. Eateries in Redmond, Issaquah, Federal Way and Jonny's favorite, 1st and Pike in the old Pike Street Bar and Grill space, followed, each multiplying the degree of our initial success.

Jan now resides in New Hampshire with her second husband and two sons. Along with vulgar riches, she's finally achieved the legitimacy she so long desired. The old girl drops by from time to time, and on those occasions never fails to thank the two of us for what she considers her salvation. Her boys, by the way, are named Scottie and Jon. Both my attorney and I think this a bit odd, then again, imitation is supposedly the most sincere form of flattery and our egos remain mollified. Jonny has assumed the persona of the brutally effective, son of a bitch lawyer who steers the company through the shark infested seas of corporate America. As for me, I'm pretty much useless—a conspicuous figurehead who lends a sense of identity to the institution. I appear in television commercials with my mom and grandmother, speak a little Polish on the radio and collect the largest paycheck of all. Jonny once explained the legal necessity for my monstrous compensation package, but I wasn't interested in his legalese. "Don't cum in a gift horse's mouth," I always say.

Chapter 4

A Day In The Life

Number one, the original West Seattle store, is the outpost of my business to which I still feel the strongest attachment. It eloquently expresses the enormous irony possible within the context of the American dream; Polish food dispensed from a Spanish colonial building into a predominantly Asian neighborhood. It was upon this stronghold of our success that Jonny, Bro and I converged with a haste born of desperation.

The dog had spent the duration of our retreat from the now forbidden city of Sea-Tac, punching buttons on the car's CD player and howling along to Pink Floyd's "Comfortably Numb," guitar solos and all. After his third time through the song, I suggested to Bro that he make an alternate selection. He stabbed absently at the stereo until The Rolling Stone's "Angie" burst to life from my expensive speaker array. His variations on "Comfortably Numb" were genius by comparison.

Jonny arrived at the restaurant in a dramatic squealing of premium vulcanized rubber two minutes after us. The angry pinging emitting from his black Lotus' engine compartment hinted at the severity of the paces he'd put the sports car through on his way to, once again, deliver me from evil of my own making. It required a combined effort to lift Bro from the Cadillac and carry him into a small office adjacent the liquor room.

On staff at the time of our unscheduled visit was

Scirocco Taco's daytime bartender, a seasoned pro I knew only as "Bonnie." She'd spent her last 14 years behind an impressive succession of bars and had grown so weary of drunks and their moronic sexual advances that she would now work only weekday lunch shifts, which in a cocktail lounge translates to 10 a.m. to 6 p.m. It pleased Bonnie to no end that her duties during those leisurely hours when liquor consumption was down and food was the going item, were more those of a waitress than a barkeep. She was content to make her tips slinging sauerkraut and sausage instead of whiskey sours. The majority of her liquor oriented obligations consisted of stocking the bar for the evening bartender, Mark—a virtuoso mixologist with the ability to prepare drinks at breakneck speed while diplomatically humoring even the most belligerent drunk.

Jonny helped me lay Bro on the office's old hide-a-bed sofa (an article of furniture which had, over the years, been utilized in capacities never intended by its manufacturer) then phoned up the bar. Bonnie answered in her curt, professional manner.

"Scirocco Taco bar, this is Bonnie."

"Hi, honey. Your ass is like a pair of farm fresh cantaloupes, probably as sweet, too. Daddy wants a taste. Papa wants to snake his nasty tongue up your ass and lick your heart—cardiolingus."

"Hi, Jonny. What's up?" Nothing shocks Bonnie, a desirable trait in a bartender.

"Listen, kid," Jonny went on, unfazed by her indifference. "Scottie and I are here in the office. Would you whip up a couple of Rusty Nails and have one of the girls bring them back? Thanks, honey. I'll have this penny-pinching dick back here..." he stabbed a thumb at me as if Bonnie could somehow see him. "...give you a raise. Bye now."

A short time later, my faculties somewhat restored by the Scotch and Drambuie, I finished relating my account of the day's events to Jonny who, to his credit, had listened thoughtfully and without interruption. I watched his eyes move from the floor, to the dog, and back again several times as he took in my story. It was several moments before he finally spoke.

"Did you do anything that would have led any of your fellow diners at The Pancake Chef to believe you were blind?"

"Oh, you mean like standing atop a table and visually scanning for a doctor, or maybe gathering up old Bro and running like a greyhound to the Cadillac?"

"I see your point," he conceded. "That leaves only one viable alternative."

"What's that?" I inquired, hope dawning weak and cool in my heart like the sun on Neptune's horizon.

"It wasn't you," Jonny stated flatly. "It was a Scottie Scirocco imposter who perpetrated this morning's ugly events. The entire, sordid affair was nothing more than a vicious act of corporate espionage staged by our hated rivals at Taco-Bueno for purpose of ruining us. It's widely known that we've cut deeply into what were once their exclusive markets. Hell, they don't give a shit that we're actually a Polish restaurant. Their problem resides in the fact that our stores look like Mexican joints. The Public had burnt out on the Taco-Bueno menu and was looking for something different. It saw a new Mexicanesque place, ducked in for an investigative dinner and, POW! Who cares if eating head cheese appetizers and czarninia (duck blood soup) has superceded pork flautas and huevos rancheros? The food is delicious. The public, fickle thing it is, swears off gas-engendering, refried, tortilla-swathed offal and begins showing up here in all its commercially viable might."

Jonny was gathering momentum—attaining the magical, hysteria induced level of subjective truth that was the hallmark of his genius. If he convinced himself it hadn't been me in that restaurant—that the person in question actually was a corporate saboteur—then he could easily convince any jury in the land of the same.

"Why don't you take Bro home," he suggested, mopping a sheen of fervor-born sweat from his forehead. "Take my car so no one sees that faggoty Cadillac of yours leaving here. I don't want any evidence of you being out and about today. After you're safely away, I'll have Hector or one of the other kitchen guys pull the Caddie around back and park it between the catering vans, safe from prying eyes. Helen can drop me by here on her way home from the office tonight. I'll drive your car back to my place and stash it in the garage." Jonny drained his Rusty Nail, produced a series of vials from his coat pocket, selected one, dispensed from it a clean line of the purest cocaine money could buy, and fortified himself for the upcoming legal brainstorming. He offered me a toot of his high dollar blow, but I politely declined. I would undertake my own anti-stress measures upon my safe arrival home.

Chapter 5

Smatterings on the Downside

Jonny's Lotus was a hoot to drive—a flat-out, run-like-hell, motherfucker of a machine that whispered idiocies.

"Faster...go faster. No need to slow down for that off ramp."

It was also, sadly, strictly a driver's car. Bro emphatically disliked the vehicle. He woke from his morphine coma as I launched the little car into the lunchtime traffic milling around the West Seattle store. No sooner had the dog realized his whereabouts than he issued a flatulence so sour it bordered criminal. I managed to locate the electric window control and ventilate the cabin before I lapsed into unconsciousness.

"Feel better?" I inquired bitterly.

Yes, thank you, he yawned. *What was the marvelous remedy you permitted that nomadic quack to administer into my veins? Horrifying though my memories of this morning are, I feel capital. Strong magic, man. Watch this.*

The shameless pig contorted his previously rigid spine, shot a rear leg skyward and made a vulgar display of licking his balls—an unnecessary, entirely over-the-top theatric undertaken for the sole purpose of illustrating his transient good health. Between rasping inhalations, the muffled sound of laughter rose from the musty recesses of the dog's loins.

"Enough already! I get the picture," I beseeched him. He had forgotten me entirely, though and expanded his undertaking to include a vigorous, self-inflicted rim job.

"Stop Goddamnit!" I entreated him a second time. "You're making me sick. Have some humility for the Christsake!" Finally, the dog relented. "Hence the term, *Animal*," I chided.

Bro sifted through the car's CD library. I watched, appalled, as a shimmering rivulet of drool descended from his jowls onto Jonny's otherwise impeccably maintained copy of Iron Maiden's *Piece of Mind* album. The dog sank luxuriously into the Lotus's brushed leather upholstery as I inserted the silver platter and punched up a track entitled, "Revelations." The song launched from the speakers with a ferocity that enhanced my appreciation of the little car, and I sang—the day's tribulation momentarily forgotten in British, heavy metal excellence.

This tune is about Saint Thomas Aquinas's sexual trans-gressions with an electric toaster prototype, Bro blurted as he relapsed into morphine delirium. *In 1510, oblivious to repeated warnings by its inventor not to do so, St. Thomas Aquinas attempted to bring the worlds of religion and sci-*

ence together by baptizing an electric toaster. The goodly, if not well-educated, saint rose to the elite ranks of martyrdom when he waded into the Jordan with the contraption and, after muttering a series of cryptic Latin incantations, submerged the appliance. To the surprise and lasting horror of the assembled multitude, St. Tom stiffened and appeared to actually steam. Dead carp rose from the dirty water and rolled languidly around the smoldering saint who vanished in a dazzling blue crackle.

Bro's great pink tongue rolled from his slackened jaws as the dog crumpled, unconscious, to the floorboard. Thank God. I had been expecting a bolt of lightning to issue from the cloudless sky and dispatch the blasphemous animal outright.

With the recalcitrant dog down for the count, matters returned to a semblance of normalcy. Only a few more blocks and we would be home. I would drop the dog onto his bed, go to market so as to stock up for our coming hiatus from public view, run by my friend Russ's house for some extraneous frivolities and hotfoot it back home before Bro ever knew I was gone.

Chapter 6

Give Us This Day Our Daily Bread and Forgive Russ His Trespasses

R uss Wilson lay steeping in a bath hot enough to kill an infant. The water's surface glistened a suspicious shade of green evincing the copious dose of Oriental bath crystals with which he had fortified it. In keeping with his long-established custom, Wilson wore his underclothes in the bath. "Never know when you might have to up and run from, or worse yet, fight off dangerous intruders," he'd explained years before when, in our friendship's fledgling days, I'd questioned him about this admittedly bizarre habit. "Ever fight naked?" he went on to ask me. "Hell, you can't begin to take yourself seriously enough to kick someone's ass. It's psychology, man. You get to intimidating some criminally psychotic Jehovah's Witness who's broken into your house with a crow bar and an issue of Watchtower, and all he sees is a shivering, naked hippie with soap in his ears and shriveled balls. No joy. Sorry circumstance, man. He'll whack you across your eyes with that magazine and chase your blind ass back into the bathroom where he'll fuck you with a shampoo bottle before slitting your throat and watching your blood run down the drain. Not me. No way."

A bottle of Bushmill's Irish whiskey—half relegated to Wilson's gut—stood sentry beside the tub. His hand dangled limply an inch above the bottle's mouth. Unique to Wilson's restroom was an easy chair upholstered in the finest, coral-blue vinyl. The chair sat just far enough from the tub to be out of splashing range. Before I could protest, Wilson was pouring me a drink. Assuring myself worse fates existed than free alcohol proffered by a mildly psychotic friend, I accepted the libation and sank into the blue-vinyl monstrosity to conduct the business about which I'd come calling.

"Dog freaked out," I began. "Let loose in what is no doubt a no shitting zone in Sea-Tac, of all places. What's worse, a waitress slipped in his offal. She might have broken her fucking neck, man. I didn't hang around to find out. We blazed like nobody's business. Jonny says the dog and I should lay low for a week or two. I've come for supplies. The usual type stuff, but I need fifty percent more than I ordinarily go in for. You see, the dog had an arthritis fit at the Pancake Chef. Bad scene, that was. There was a silver lining to the madness, however. Understand, I thought the hairy bastard was dying and staged a scene for purpose of flushing a physician from the crowd. Naturally, one materialized. He was a charlatan, though, and shot the dog up with a king's ransom of morphine, probably a good five times more than was absolutely necessary. I've given this some thought. It stands to reason that this alleged doctor deals, in the course of his alleged practice, with drug dosages appropriate to human patients. Hence, his veterinary faux pas. But who gives a shit anyway. The fact of the matter is, Bro mellowed right out—no outward traces of pain, no bitching about his hips. He seemed...hell, healthy."

Wilson listened intently to my tale of Hippocratic depravity between periodic submersions. His expression shifted like the swirls and eddies of his bath as I spun the yarn and, more than once, he clucked his tongue in what I assumed was amazement.

I concluded my story and waited tensely for my friend's commentary. He stared at me for a long moment through THC-reddened eyes before speaking.

"You're going to use your beautiful, beautiful money to purchase my drugs with full intent to administer them to your dog for reason of curing his arthritis? That's hard core, Scirocco. I'm moved, man. My heart bleeds like Jesus' fallen arches."

Wilson rose from the emerald waters of his bath and slogged across the bathroom's expensive tile flooring to an ornate towel rack from which he selected a white, terry-cloth robe. The garment's back had emblazoned upon it a botanically accurate, needlepoint rendition of a cannabis leaf while up front, the lapels sported matching embroidery.

"Follow," he ordered.

We descended a flight of wooden stairs that led down into Wilson's cavernous basement. Fluorescent sunlamps stood sentinel over a subterranean marijuana farm that knew no equal. Electric timers tripped far away solenoids that, in turn, released short bursts of misty rainfall from overhead plumbing. Specialized sensors in the farm's fragrant soil monitored pH levels and added fertilizer accordingly. Wilson's mature plants were absolutely magnificent—horticultural triumphs whose stalks drooped visibly under the prodigious weight of bunches of slick, heavy leaves. His best specimens would never know the pipe. Instead, they were retained for seed. Genetic purity was the foundation upon which Wilson had built his underground empire, an empire that had steadily expanded to include numerous, full-service divisions that provided the discriminating connoisseur of top-shelf pharmaceuticals an eclectic variety of pills, potions and powders. Wilson had overseen and personally guided the early careers of several of Seattle's drug dealing elite. His protegés included "Two-Fist Willie," White Center's most infamous narcotics felon whose title was allegedly bestowed in honor of the man's peculiar tendency to shamelessly masturbate while high on ecstasy. The fronts of Willie's trousers were supposedly so stained with semen that he took to wearing chaps so as to be better able to unload where and when he pleased without having to wear the evidence of his transgressions. Wilson used to joke that Willie's first piece of ass had come after he'd gotten his hand drunk. Initially, Willie was terribly humiliated by the unwelcome public awareness his habit won him. Years later, having come to *grips* with his unique social stature, Willie began to openly joke about his tendencies.

"I woke up in the middle of the night and found a fist in my bed," he would say. "I figured, shit, I better fuck this thing before it beats the hell out of me."

Sadly, Willie's tastes in pharmaceuticals began ranging to the extreme. On Christmas Eve, 1990, Willie was found dead in an adult arcade. He had apparently ingested a huge overdose of PCP, then retired to a jerk-off booth where he masturbated with such fury that he tore his penis from its mooring ligament. Reliable sources report that he ran, shrieking and bloody, from the video booth into the establishment's front area where he confronted the attendant and, dangling his mutilated organ in the chap's face, demanded, "What'll you give me for it?"

The horrified attendant, mute with fear, staggered backward into a display of anatomically accurate dildo's. Willie perceived the man's action as an indication that, though unwilling to pay cash money for the severed penis, the attendant might consider a trade. Willie consented. Snatching up one of the faux phalli, he zipped it into the fly of his blood-spattered chinos and returned to the video booth where he spent the last moments of his life endeavoring to coax emission from the rubber rod. Willie died from loss of blood, bitterly disappointed about having been suckered into a bad trade.

Another of Wilson's noteworthy apostles was "Pitbull Tim" of Sumner. Tim had been nothing but a small-time dope fiend who had the foresight to purchase a handful of select seed from Wilson in the early part of 1988. From those few seeds, he cultivated a cannabis crop that rivaled Wilson's own. Tim lacked spiritual unity with his plants, though, and to this day, his product lags somewhat behind Wilson's in smoothness.

To guard his lucrative enterprise, Tim retained the services of a white and tan pitbull that he had raised from a pup. The animal, it was said, had been weaned on the flesh of live kittens that Tim procured on the bootleg from a client/girlfriend who worked weekends at the Pierce County animal shelter. The dog was reputedly so fierce that once Tim set the animal on an intruder or deadbeat customer, it could only be subdued by the insertion of a finger into its rectum.

Even Jan attributed her early success to Wilson's tutelage and encouragement. For years, after she'd emerged from beneath his wing, she continued corresponding with him regularly.

Treading the shadow of this icon of the local drug cul-

ture, I descended into the inauspicious basement from which he had amassed a fortune against which even my riches seemed trivial. The sheer enormity of Wilson's inventory was staggering and I marveled at it openly. He instructed me to stay put and disappeared into the darkness—a Minotaur into his labyrinth. Wilson returned a short while later carrying an unremarkable satchel that I knew contained ten, maybe fifteen-thousand dollars worth of his wares. I produced from my jacket a manila envelope containing ten one-thousand-dollar bills, a pair of courtside Sonics tickets and a $100 gift certificate redeemable at any Scirocco Taco location.

"That's only the customary payment," I intoned, inclining my head toward the envelope. "I'll wire you five more this afternoon."

An introspective look played across Wilson's face.

"No, don't sweat it," he said, stroking his beard thoughtfully. "Tell you what," he went on after a moment. "You might be tapping a whole new market for me, Scottie. When I think of my well-to-do clients and their dogs, cats, pot bellied pigs and God knows what else all high…together…it makes a kind of intrinsic sense. Yeah, you take that five grand and buy your mother something."

I was just beginning to voice my appreciation of his generosity when the shrewd fucker tasked me.

"I would ask a favor in lieu of payment, though."

"What's that?" I asked.

"Watch the dog," he answered. "Record his reactions to different drugs. Keep track of his dosages, times of administration. You know…did he take the dope right after he woke up? Did he take it with coffee? That kind of shit. Write it all down in a journal that you can hand over to me in a few weeks. If the results of your field work look even the least bit promising, I'm going to branch out into new markets. I have a feeling, Scottie—good tomorrows. I feel it, man."

At the time, his terms seemed well worth the five grand

I was saving and I agreed with them enthusiastically. We closed the deal with a handshake. It was then I noticed how luxuriously soft Wilson's hands are—lots of moisturizing baths. He led me back to his bathroom where I watched, fascinated, as he drained the water from the tub. It wasn't the idea of him discarding practically new bath water that I found bizarre. It was the way he spoke to the departing fluid.

"Go in peace to caress and serve others," he called into the drain as the last of the emerald water swirled away. "Into this plumbing I commend my essence." Wilson's nonsensical variations on the Catholic mass troubled me somehow.

"What in the fuck are you doing, man?" I asked, no longer able to contain myself.

"The water absorbs my *Ka*. That's Egyptian for *spirit*," he explained. "I only sit in a bath long enough for it to receive my Ka, and for me to assimilate the Ka of the last person around whom those particular waters circulated. Its like a big, hydraulic communion. You should try it."

"I jerk off in the tub," I fired back. "I even shit in it once. So long, man."

To this day, Wilson won't admit that he hesitated for just a moment before beginning to draw a fresh Ka.

I made my way back to the Lotus, all the while contemplating the task with which my friend had burdened me.

Chapter 7

The Ball Shudders

My trip home was blessedly free of incident. I returned to find Bro exactly as I'd left him. The swine lay in a puddle of his own drool. I winced at the realization that he'd rolled upon and ruined one of my favorite shirts, a development with which I was not at all happy. Seating myself at the foot of my bed, I opened the satchel with which Wilson had presented me. Yet again, I found myself dazzled by the man's pharmaceutical prudence. Contained in the parcel was a collection of complementary poisons that only a true connoisseur could have compiled. Wilson had supplemented two bags of his legendary marijuana with 100 or so mescaline tablets, two sheets of the black acid, a glass vile containing 12 or 15 grams of cocaine, a square of folded aluminum foil that I knew contained a wad of raw opium, a couple hundred 20/20's (speed), enough hash to flat-line a horse and finally, a bottle of medical oxygen complete with respirator assembly—this last item included for purpose of intensifying the effects of a few of the drugs. Wilson was nothing, if not thorough.

Play some music, Archibald.

Bro was coming to.

"Who?" I inquired.

You, cock snot! Play me some fucking music before I bite your Goddamn skull. I swear to God, I'll latch on to the back of your head and hang there like a remora until you die. Now let's have some music!

He was in a bit of a snit—poor bastard. I'd seen him this way before. When the pain got really bad Bro had a tendency to become short. The morphine must have been wearing off. Pacifying the beast was paramount. I fumbled for an LP. Black Sabbath's *Heaven and Hell* was at the top of the stack. The record seemed a good choice—introspective but not too self-important. I knew the dog considered the two albums Sabbath cut with Ronnie James Dio to be the band's finest. Bro was an avid Dio fan and would happily have paid a large sum of my cash money for a recording of the singer crooning on the toilet. The music seemed to placate him. Forsaking his ranting, Bro watched with quiet curiosity as I rooted through the satchel for narcotics.

So began the most bizarre experiment in cross-genus cohabitation ever endeavored.

Chapter 8

I Like To Be Here
When I Can

November 21st, year unimportant:

Rain is to Seattle as is sun to the Sahara. Most years the rains begin in October and continue doggedly until the following June. Bro had been lying in a ground floor bay window for two days. He refused food and would take only Scotch on the rocks. He was not sober. He was dangerous. Confinement had not agreed with him. The relentless rain had aggravated the situation. Bro suffered, as did four in ten Seattleites, from Seasonal Affective Disorder, or S.A.D, a condition whose sufferers experienced irrational, severe depression as the result of long-term, dismal weather. Physicians who tout the disease and offer bizarre and costly treatments for it profess that exposure to sunlight triggers a physiological response similar to that elicited by stimulant drugs—nature's way of saying *up and at 'em.* Denied sunlight, however, the body's processes slow. The resultant depression is apparently of sufficient severity to foster Seattle's nation-leading, per capita suicide rate. S.A.D. indeed.

Personally, I thought it was a bunch of shit. The dog considered my opinion meaningless, though, and continued his descent into hypochondria. Incessant lamentation echoed through the house. Cries of, *My God, my God, why have you forsaken me?* and *The tragedy of life is its tendency to endure,* somersaulted, one over the other, until it seemed I'd taken up residence in New Testament Jerusalem. My repeated attempts to coax Bro from the window had met with failure. Neither board games nor billiards, nor even photos of wanton bitches clipped from back issues of *Dog Fancy* had succeeded in dragging Bro from his melancholy.

It was time. I retreated to my upstairs bedroom and pulled the sacred satchel, the ark of mine and Wilson's covenant, from a high shelf in my closet. I yanked sternly at the zipper, in a hurry to access the pockets and compartments that held in their hallowed recesses the stuff of street corner sacraments. Annoyed as I was with his recent behavior, I decided to begin the dog's therapy with a drug sure to reek havoc on his innards. Snatching up a pair of mescaline tablets, I smiled knowingly and, dropping the little beauties into my hip pocket, made my way back downstairs with a refreshing sense of purpose.

"Bro! Snap to, big boy. I've got your arthritis pills," I chanted gleefully. He hated the humiliation of having to swallow pills with my assistance and would likely be too angry to notice the mickey I was about to slip him. The mescaline was similar in both size and color to his Arthritis medication. This wouldn't be too difficult.

"Come on, old man," I repeated, feigning irritation. "Take your medicine. I don't give a good goddamn if you die up there in that window. Just don't think you're going to load me up with guilt for not doing my part to ensure your continued, miserable existence. Now eat your fucking pills."

Nazi, he grumbled, fighting to straighten himself from the contortions of disease. *Your grandfather was probably Himmler's dietitian—both a Nazi and a failure.*

"And your grandmother was the explosives dog who cleared Pan Am 500," I countered. "Now take your goddamn pill."

He snarled at me and then, in his peculiar fashion, obediently opened his tartar-ridden maw to accept the medication. I moved like a mongoose. Snapping one mescaline tablet under his nose, I waited the half-second I knew it would take him to gag on the unexpected inhalation of chemical dust. As I'd expected, the beast's eyes glassed over with a sheen of tears and his jaws swung open in a desperate attempt to gulp untainted air. Taking quick but careful aim, I popped the second tablet into the pink horror of his throat.

In humans, the effects of mescaline are perceptible within minutes. In dogs, they are shockingly immediate. Bro's body coiled upon itself, contracting with gruesome intensity. His eyes bulged from their sockets and long streamers of mucous erupted from his dilated nostrils. The fur along his neck and shoulders stood on end and his tail swung pendulously to and fro. Without warning, the dog's entire sympathetic nervous system crapped out and he slid limply to the living room's carpeted floor. I was afraid he might loose his bowels and bladder so I gathered him in my arms and carried him downstairs to the laundry room.

Tense moments ensued. Bro hung suspended, teetering between the mundane and the surreal as his body fought to reestablish chemical equilibrium. Then, as suddenly as the episode of physical mayhem had raged to life, it subsided. An expression of pure contentment dawned on Bro's haggard features and I felt his vibe change for the better.

Morning, Scottie!, he beamed.

This was enormously disconcerting. The dog never, absolutely *never*, called me by my first name.

How's for you and me go back topside and have a drink. I'm parched, man.

"Sure Bro...come on. I'll give you a hand," I stammered, too horrified to refuse him.

No need, Scottie, he beamed, *I feel capital!*

An astounding thing happened then. Rising from the laundry room floor, Bro straightened to his full height and shook. He shook and shook until I was sure he was in the throes of a death spasm. He shook until dust and dander that had benn accumulating in his coat for years uncounted filled the air around him—and still he shook. Slobber flew from his slapping jowls and flecked my expensive washer and drier as the animal shook himself with a vigor he'd not known since puppy-hood. His shake complete, Bro trotted out the door and around the corner, then bounded like a jack rabbit up the stairs.

Lord have mercy, Scottie! I heard him say from the kitchen. *I know goddamn well that wasn't Arthritis medicine you fed me. For a second I thought you were offing me. It isn't like I haven't been a regular prick lately. But Christ, man. You've cured me. You're a shittin' neoclassic Doctor Doolittle. Come up here and have a drink. Hell, you can even drink that sailing-ship rot you consistently mistake for Scotch. I, however, will be having the Glenlevit. Your last bitch of a girlfriend; I remember how she used to complain that my Glenlevit cost twenty-eight dollars a bottle. I say, fuck her. That rat-piss perfume of hers cost one hundred-fifty dollars an ounce and still smelled like day-old shit. A curse on her. Scottie, are you coming up, old boy? Come punch the numbers on this phone Scottie. I think I'll have a mime. Yes, that would be nice. Phone up whatever agency it is that contracts mimes. I'd like one for the afternoon. I should like to see him...or her, I can't tell the fucking difference, I should very much like to see the androgynous mime person climb an imaginary rope or negotiate an escape from one of those sinister, invisible cubes.*

Chapter 9

But is it Art?

Later that afternoon, a box van belonging to the Marceau West agency pulled up to the house's main gate. I punched a code into the telephone and watched on a closed-circuit television monitor as the vehicle maneuvered down my inclined drive. Marveling at my inability to deny the dog his desires, I hung up the phone and made ready to greet our contractually obligated mime.

The van squealed to a halt in front of the main house and, amidst a sighing of old leaf springs and burble of FM light rock, disgorged its lone occupant—a Mr. Devin Wick, pantomime artist of questionable origin. Mr. Wick's costume was traditional mime fare. His face paint, however, was a different matter entirely. Displaying a master's touch with pancake and grease pencils, Wick had made himself up in striking blacks and whites to resemble a horrible, cackling skull. Gumless teeth, outlined over his lips and curving back nearly to his ears, leered in a lunatic smile that lent a sinister air to Wick's otherwise inane profession.

I signed the invoice with which Wick presented me and, without a word uttered between us, we entered the house. I led Wick to the living room where Bro had seated himself on an expensive ottoman in eager anticipation of the afternoon's entertainment. A hint of what might have been flattery played across Wick's skeletal features as the dog howled with delight at his arrival.

I seated myself in the lounge chair behind Bro and made ready to recreate myself. Mr. Wick bowed low before us and, as he rose, stopped so violently that for a moment I thought he actually *had* hit his head on something. I applauded when the moment's confusion passed, and Bro wagged his tail madly as Wick examined the invisible treachery against which he had feigned collision. Satisfied that the unseen obstacle necessitated no further attention, Wick endeavored to push an immovable object across the room before stopping, exhausted, to rest against an invisible pillar. His antics bored me.

Seeking my amusement elsewhere, I glanced at Bro. It occurred to me suddenly that the mescaline would be wearing off shortly. Excusing myself, I hurried upstairs to procure additional medication for my disease beleaguered companion. I had just returned the satchel to its shelf and was slipping two fresh mescaline tablets into my shirt pocket when Hell broke loose in the living room.

Hurriedly concluding my covert business, I flew back downstairs with reckless haste. The scene I arrived upon was unspeakably bad. Wick had ascended my dining room table. This in itself horrified me insomuch as the table, unseen beneath the expensive cloth with which I'd tastefully covered it, was a fragile, glass affair.

The dog was deep and dirty in an arthritic rage. He limped, snarling and foaming like a warm Guinness around the table. His coat bristled and the twin rows of the dog's formidable dentition flashed in authentic, wild pig fashion.

Come down you fraud, you weasly cunt! Bro demanded *I'm going to gnaw off your leg and knock up your thigh!*

The dog's head snapped around. He'd heard me. My damnable boots had squeaked across the kitchen's hardwood floor as I maneuvered around the island for a better look at the incredible proceedings.

"Bro! What the hell are you doing?" I demanded. "Don't you think we're in quite enough trouble already?"

Mr. Wick removed himself a step from the unpleasant precipice of wetting his costume as my presence drew the animal's attention away from him. It was clear from the look that played across his skull that my irrationally logical approach to canine discipline confounded him.

"Shoot it," he whimpered. "Make it stop. I didn't *mean* anything. I wasn't thinking."

"Calm yourself, Bro," I went on, heedless of the idiot mime.

Wick all but wept with relief as the dog limped from the table and followed me back into the living room.

I'm telling you, Scottie, the dog began once we were in private. *The man is a fraud. The minute you left the room he sat his kleptomaniacal ass on the piano bench and began casing the joint. He was finger fucking your brass tic-tac-toe set when I snarled at him. You know, just to let him know that it wasn't intermission yet. That's when it happened.*

"What happened?" I demanded. This seemed serious.

He kicked me.

"What!" I was outraged and Jonny was only a prepro-grammed, speed dial button away.

I couldn't believe it either, Scottie, Bro continued. *He was quicker than lightning. His foot shot out like a cobra and caught me in the hip. Whatever it was you gave me is keeping the crazy pain at bay, but my damn hindquarter feels like broken glass.*

"Here, eat these," I commanded, popping the two mescaline tablets down his hatch.

Bless you, he said before lapsing into a better place.

Black rage descended on me like a disease. I could still see the abusive mime holding his squeamish pose atop the dining room table—the *glass* dining room table. He maintained his place at the dead center of the expensive furnishing and watched intently as the dog slumped, unconscious.

"Mr. Wick…" I called.

"Did you poison him?" came the cur's answer. "Give him some more. He might come around and attack you. For godsakes, be careful, man!"

Wick jumped as Bro let out a contented snort. Instinctively, the revolting man retreated to the far edge of the table that had become his sanctuary. Without warning,

the heavy glass table top somersaulted up and struck the stupefied mime full in his bony face. The safety glass held together nicely. The same could not be said for Wick. His skeletal visage exploded in technicolor reds that were made even more dramatic by the chalky white background against which they were displayed. I watched fascinated as the painted teeth split and bled lustily onto my hardwood floor.

Good thing you didn't carpet in there, Bro commented as Wick fell, unconscious, to the lacquered deck.

I ran upstairs and fetched a good dose of cocaine. As resentful as I felt about wasting premium product, I had no choice. I meted out, then held perhaps a half tablespoonful of the powerful dust under Wick's bloody, bubbling nostrils. For a moment, I thought the man dead, that was until the cocaine began disappearing in conjunction with his rasping inhalations. Planting toxicological evidence was unsavory work, but I knew Jonny could use the tactical advantage should he have to clear me of any liability incurred over the course of this disastrous afternoon.

Three hours later the last of the police and paramedics had departed, leaving only a tow truck to drag Wick's van from my property. Responding officers had done their job and collected blood samples from the traumatized mime after I reported his behavior prior to the unfortunate accident as having been strange and erratic.

"He seemed paranoid," I told Officer Pasteur. The poor cop appeared to have been seriously burned at some point in his life and looked lucky to have survived.

"Yes, sir. I see," Pasteur responded curtly. "We'll have the lab look at the samples taken. We found a half gram or so of cocaine in his van. Looks like a fairly cut and dry case. If we need you, we'll be in touch. I've got your statement here, so that's all for now. Good afternoon, Mr. Scirocco."

"Thanks Officer," I nodded. "Watch yourself out there."

He doffed his hat in acknowledgment and even pet Bro's wiry head on his way out.

"Nice guy," I thought. I resented having to fool him but desperate times…

Nice guy, Bro spoke up. *Too bad we had to lead him on like that.*

"Yeah, I was just thinking the same thing," I added. "Felt kind of good to fuck up Mister animal abuser though."

You said it, man. Bro beamed in agreement. *Planting that dope was good, but the way you maneuvered the mime into traumatizing himself, that was genius.*

"Thank you," I beamed, offering a small bow.

The phone rang, shattering our moment of relative calm. It was my attorney.

"Jonny! Yes, everything is cool." It took me little more than five minutes to relate the day's tale.

Jonny laughed out loud at my account of the afternoon's drama. His mirth, I think, was part sincere amusement, and part product of his heartfelt relief that I hadn't exacerbated my already dicey position.

"No more people from the out-fucking-side," Jonny emphatically instructed before hanging up.

"Okay, okay," I agreed, but the line had already gone dead.

What did he say? The animal was tense with apprehension.

"He said no more mimes."

Oh, that's okay, he sighed, visibly relaxing. *Fuck the mimes. They have no real sense of style anyway. Let's get some strippers in here.*

"Actually, he said no outsiders of any kind for the remainder of our little sabbatical."

None? Bro demanded in utter outrage. *Not even the grocery delivery boy?*

"I suppose that would be all right," I conceded. "Just no one inside the house, socially or otherwise."

Aw shit! I need a drink. What's this poison you've been feeding me anyway, man?

I twitched a couple of times, then cracked under the direct pressure.

"It's mescaline."

Hmmm...I like it. Is it from Wilson?

"Yes. I picked it up yesterday while you were sleeping off the morphine that doctor shot you with at the Pancake Chef, or don't you remember?"

Of course I remember, shit-wit, he fired back. *Mescaline, huh? Yes, I really do like it. Besides, if it's from Wilson it must be okay, right?*

"Right," I agreed.

What else did he give you?

"Come see." I waited patiently as the beast hobbled up the stairs. I followed him to my room and the satchel.

Chapter 10

All Along The Watchtower

Eight hits of high octane, black acid had dealt me a trip so stellar I was beginning to wonder if I would ever come down. Four hits had done the dog a similar disservice. I had used crude junkie math to determine our respective dosages; one hit for every 20 pounds of body weight. At 185 pounds, I had been conservative with my ration. In the interest of pure science, however, I had overdosed Bro by a full hit, based on his 70 pounds of limping insolence.

The dog had sat motionless for about 30 minutes, absorbed in some introspective ritual. Suddenly, moved by forces imperceptible to me, he sat bolt upright and ran halfway up a wood paneled wall before flopping grotesquely backward and crumpling on the floor. I was relatively sure he had killed himself and was feverishly formulating an explanation by which to appease Wilson when he righted himself and, seizing the satchel in his jaws, retreated to the bedroom's far corner. There, in the weak light of a reading lamp, he endeavored fruitlessly to dig a hole.

"What in God's name are you doing?" I demanded.

He relented just long enough for me to see the look of genuine terror that had fixed itself, like a bad Mardi Gras mask, to his features.

They're coming, Scottie! he whimpered. *They're on to us, man! I smell them! I can hear the pages of their Bibles whispering like conspiratorial priests. Is the gate closed?* He jumped up onto the bed and strained for a look out the window. *Holy fuck, Scottie, you irresponsible shrew, the damn thing is wide open! Give me the phone!* He seized the receiver in his jaws and shook it as if murdering a rabbit. *It isn't working! Help me!*

The dog foamed and fell from the bed. Mesmerized by his errant behavior, I ventured a half-hearted look outside. To my surprise the unsettling specter of two young women, pleasantly attired and a somewhat over-wholesome, appeared cresting the hill leading down from the arterial.

"Bro, don't you bail on me," I snarled, seizing the beast by his throat. "Who are they? You weren't kidding. I forgot about that nose and those ears of yours. Who are they I say?" My throttling dragged him back from the edge of the abyss. "Talk, you junkie fuck," I screamed. "Talk or I swear to god, I'm going to shoot you so full of heroin that your liver and kidneys will unzip your gut and go looking for a more hospitable place to live."

The doorbell rang. Time seemed to have compressed.

The sharp metallic report shocked the dog into a semblance of consciousness. Slobbering copiously, he rolled his eyes toward mine and croaked out,

Watch Tower.

"Holy fucking shit," I cursed. "Jehovah's Witnesses." I wasn't sure whether I'd thought or actually spoken the words aloud.

The door bell rang a second time implying the latter. Bro's weight went dead in my hands as fear and pharmacy alike sapped his will to remain coherent. The bastard's luck stupefied me. I left him lying on the floor and made my clumsy way toward the front door. My attempt to compose myself on the way down met with utter failure. A last minute look in the foyer mirror was anything but encouraging. Resigning myself to whatever sorry fate awaited, I counted to three and swung open the door.

The blast of cool air and the smell of a world made tolerably clean by incessant rain had a momentary revitalizing effect.

"Hello, ladies," I beamed. The pair seemed taken back by my enthusiastic reception.

"Good afternoon, sir," the older of the two (who herself could not have been more than 25) took the initiative. "My name is Sandra, and this is Jennifer. We were wondering if perhaps you could spare us a few moments of your time this fine day?"

"Why certainly, ladies," I smiled, my confidence taking an upswing. You're not going to try selling me Tupperware or marital aids, are you?" I put special emphasis on *marital aids* and got a satisfying round of nervous giggles for my effort.

"No sir. Nothing like that. What we're offering is absolutely free," Sandra countered in an obvious hurry to return to more neutral ground.

"Good, good," I agreed. "I like that kind of thing. Please…" I ushered them into the kitchen and put on a pot of coffee. I knew die-hard Mormons were forbidden to drink caffeine and was reasonably sure Jehovah's Witnesses operated under similar constraints. I sensed a deliciously savage mind game afoot. If the ladies refused the coffee, they appeared rude and in their faith-distorted minds ran a good chance of disenchanting what they perceived a potential convert. Of course, they wouldn't want to encumber their pending sales pitch by explaining to me at this early juncture that coffee is on the *thou-shalt-not* list because a front-loading of too many dogmatic restrictions made for bad business. On the other hand, if they acquiesced to social norms and accepted the coffee, they compromised their own belief system. A transgression they could, of course, rationalize by considering it a self-sacrificing gesture given up in the throes of spreading the word. Either way, the women were forced into a spiritual dilemma and I got a cup of my own, fabulous coffee. I loved psychological maneuvering; life with the cunning animal had made me an adept.

I ventured a look at my guests over the screaming of an electric coffee grinder. They had busied themselves with the fetching of a cumbersome bunch of literature from a well-traveled valise. I thought of my own bag upstairs. With diabolical subtlety, the acid tweaked and tuned my mind in such a way that I envisioned my satchel sprouting legs, a head and twelve or so hideous, hairy tits. In my mind's eye, I saw it raise its hackles and descend the stairs, jaws flashing, trailing runny shit. I watched helpless as it sauntered into the kitchen and confronted the two women who shrieked and ran, panic stricken, into the bathroom where they dropped to their knees before the commode and prayed for deliverance from the meandering evil. Undaunted, the satchel pounced on and devoured the women's bag in a series of grunts and belches so terrifying that the younger of the two, Jennifer, if memory served, opened the toilet, discarded her shoes, stepped both dainty feet into the bowl and frantically tried flushing herself to safety. My satchel, in the meantime, ended its repast and squatted over a pit it had excavated in the hardwood floor. A sound, a horrible, terrifying sound went up from the monster as it shit a long rope of Dixie-Cups. These were gaudily decorated with portraits of Jesus and other Biblical heavyweights. The beast nuzzled my leg before trekking upstairs and, once again, becoming inanimate.

"Sir? Would you happen to have any sugar?"

"Jesus Christ," I marveled. I'd brewed and served the

coffee by proxy. It even looked as if the women were going to drink it. The situation was developing more nicely than I'd dared dream.

"Sir?" Sandra repeated.

"Yes, of course," I stammered. "How positively rude of me." I fetched sugar and, raising my cup, proposed a toast to my guests. "Peace, love, beauty and enlightenment to you, Sheiks of Middian." I burned a lip trying to conceal my laughter behind the cup. "Fill it to the rim with the rich paste of quim," the drugs blurted. Again, the humor escaped them. These girls had obviously been involved with their religious scene far too long.

"Now what exactly is this remarkable, not to mention absolutely free commodity you two are here to sell me? Are you positively sure it isn't marital aids? Because if it is, I should tell you right now that I never purchase anything without a test drive or at least an elaborate...shall we say, demonstration." The lewd overture dripped with innuendo and I wondered how close I was to alienating the girls.

"No sir. Certainly not!" Sandra blurted. She was doing a phenomenal job maintaining her focus. Across the table, Jennifer's pleasant features had grown distorted, a look of supreme repugnance spreading across them like smoke. She raised her coffee cup to her dainty mouth with jerky motions of impending panic and, as inconspicuously as she could, spit the sip she had taken back into the mug.

"Dear, sweet me," she lamented. "I am so very sorry, sir."

"Call me Scottie, Jennifer."

Her eyes filled with tears. "Mr. Scottie, I've never been so embarrassed in all of my life. Please, please forgive me for saying so, but I don't think that was sugar you brought from the cupboard, sir."

It was true that I'd filled the sugar bowl hastily. It was also true that my pantry was really more of a small closet in which I kept everything from breakfast cereal to cleaning solutions. It was becoming slowly evident that I had inadvertently pioneered the use of Saniflush as a confection.

"Jesus holy shit Christ!" I screamed. "Don't drink anymore of that stuff. It's *poison*! Dear God, how could I have been so stupid! What could I have been thinking? Please, let me take those." I hastily retrieved the coffee cups and replaced them with three cans of Pepsi. I at least couldn't screw that up.

To their credit, the women took the mishap in stride. We adjourned to the front room where Sandra launched into a polished presentation during which she endeavored to sell me a neatly packaged, all-purpose, all-season, user-friendly deity. I tried humoring her but succeeded only in horrifying the poor woman with my from-the-hip paraphrasing of her carefully composed arguments. I'd read once that the most effective way to encourage a speaker is to paraphrase their central ideas. Doing so allegedly assures him or her that effective communication is taking place. In keeping with this theory, I summarized Sandra's thoughts as follows:

"I understand, Sandra. You're saying that God the Father sent his only begotten son to the Romans to negotiate the acquisition of a southern suburb of Rome proper that would fit projected needs for a future Papal city. When it was explained to Pontius Pilate, who was in actuality a real estate broker, that the negotiator's Father planned to one day overthrow the empire and establish a kingdom of His own, the judicious Roman had no choice but to have the flower-child prototype crucified. Treason was heavy shit to the Romans. Just ask Bob Guccione."

Poor Sandra sighed audibly and was collecting her disgruntled thoughts for a second assault on my paganism when Jennifer interrupted.

"Mr. Scottie," she meekly interjected. "I'm sorry to be a bother, but would you happen to have a few aspirin or something to that effect? I'm afraid that coffee has made me a bit woozy."

87

DOC SOLOMMEN

"Yes, of course. Please, pardon me," I muttered, genuinely concerned. I left the room in search of some medication suitable for the presumed ailment—poisoning. Around the corner and up the stairs I vaulted until, finally, I stood inventorying my medicine cabinet: Nyquil, Listerine, and some Midol one of my hemorrhaging ex's had willed me spilled from the shelves, but I saw nothing with which to stem the sinister symptoms of acute toilet bowl cleanser poisoning. I needed something better, something powerful. I could hear Grace Slick crooning her way through "White Rabbit" and cursed my medicinal inadequacies. Choking back a wave of blind panic, I redoubled my search for the figurative pharmaceutical Tommy gun that would keep young Jennifer firmly entrenched in the land of the living—a chemical agent that would curtail the physiological freak out that was moving relentlessly down the pike.

Desperation breeds idiocy. I fetched the satchel from the closet and withdrew from it the folded aluminum foil packet containing the raw opium. Racing back to the medicine cabinet, I popped two Midol tablets from their plastic packaging and slathered them with as much of the sticky black paste as would readily adhere to their gel-coat. Palming the doctored tablets, I descended the stairs praying that Jennifer wouldn't examine the medication too closely before swallowing it.

Sandra sat patiently on my piano bench, her ankles crossed like a good missionary girl, as Jennifer gratefully accepted and swallowed the two tablets without so much as a glance at them. My assurance that they were simple aspirin apparently adequate.

For the next 15 minutes I endured Sandra's oration—the lion's share of my attention riveted to Jennifer, who had grown surprisingly placid. "Pray with me, Scottie. Won't you?" Sandra suddenly invited. It seemed she'd fallen under the impression that I'd made some headway on my journey toward her god. Before I could protest, Sandra grasped my right hand and Jennifer, roused by her friend's subtle prompting, had taken my left. The two lowered their eyes as Sandra began.

"Father in Heaven, look with mercy on Your son, Scottie, who this day has taken the first difficult steps on his way back to You, Almighty God. Grant him the strength his spiritual travels shall require for through You, all things are possible. This we ask through Christ, our Lord."

There was a pregnant silence during which, I now understand, I was supposed to say *Amen*. Not knowing that at the time, however, I continued the prayer, thinking it was my turn to convey my sentiments unto the Lord.

"Magnificent God," I began. "Spew not Thine righteous venom down onto the vermin of the world, among whose numbers I count myself. Rage not in Thine Heaven at the shortcomings of Your impudent manservant, Scottie. Yea, though Thee Thyself hast spoken through Thine son that, 'It is easier for a camel to pass through the eye of a needle than for a rich man to enter into the kingdom of Heaven.' I know that I shall penetrate the camel's eye and enter into Kingdom come, where every needle spews not camel, but horse. This we ask through Joe Camel, whose Smokin Joe's Suzuki factory team ran respectably during the 1996 super-bike season yet failed to impress You, Almighty God, who are oh, so lickety-split fast... Amen."

Sandra choked back a wave of nausea as I finished with what I thought was a degree of aplomb. Jennifer, surprisingly, was completely enamored by my impromptu monologue.

"Bravo, you pagan swine!" she exclaimed, leaping from her chair into my arms.

Sandra waxed Procol Harem's whiter shade of pale and appeared to come perilously close to swooning. She gripped the sides of the piano bench she was sitting on and, after a moment of straining effort, found the composure to address the developing situation.

"Thank you, Scottie," she managed between wheezes. "You've taken a very large and important step toward your soul's salvation. I'm sure you're exhausted now. Jennifer and I will take our leave of you and come calling next Sunday." She spun and shot her colleague a stern look. "Come, Jennifer."

Tension mounted as Jennifer, her eyes glazed over and fixed on my physical person, failed to respond.

"Jennifer!" Sandra repeated with a marked increase in hostility.

But young Jennifer had traveled beyond verbiage's power of retrieval. She had been practicing abstinence for too long. All it had taken was a bit of pharmaceutical free-forming to rid her of inhibition. I winced uncomfortably as Jennifer went on clinging to me in an admittedly flattering, but by and large disquieting way. Under different circum-stances, I would have welcomed her attentions. As things stood, however, her advances too closely resembled desper-ation.

Sandra's hand appeared in my peripheral vision. It descended from on high, fastening itself firmly to Jennifer's shoulder. It was obvious Sandra intended to remove her cohort from me, the premises and, perhaps ultimately, the Church. Driven to even loftier heights of arousal by the added human touch, Jennifer turned to face her partner. I felt her small hand move from my left buttock and watched, slack jawed, as it casually reached out and cupped one of Sandra's breasts.

"Spank me, mother, and give me the enema," Jennifer cooed. "I need punishment *and* purging."

The former request had a conspicuously different effect on Sandra than it did me. Reeling in revulsion, Sandra snatched up Jennifer's Bible and caché of literature and, in tones of barely contained hysteria, performed a field excommunication before bolting out the front door like a mare from a burning barn. I, on the other hand, found

Jennifer's proposal intriguing and, extracting myself from her embrace, excused myself to go searching for my home enema kit and surgical gloves.

It took me less than a minute to locate my dainties. I returned to the living room to find Jennifer casually perusing my extensive LP collection. She had become fascinated by the cover art of Emerson Lake and Palmer's *Brain Salad Surgery* album. Realizing I'd returned, Jennifer returned the record to its place on the shelf and refocused her attention on me.

"Mr. Scottie, can we do this?" She coyly asked, presenting AC/DC's *If You Want Blood...* album, the cover photo of which is a real shocker. The band's lead guitarist is depicted reeling backward into the lead singer and has, protruding from his abdomen, the body and partial neck of an electric guitar—a Gibson SG, I think. A hideous glut of blood erupts from the resulting wound.

Ms. Jennifer's expression of interest in living out the grotesque fantasy image polluted my amorous interest in her with thoughts of self-preservation.

"Yes, Scottie. This is what I want," Jennifer insisted. "I've so much wasted time to make up for!" She began to shed article after article of conservative clothing. "I want you to forego my pussy and stick your cock right into my heart." Her surprisingly alluring brassiere whispered to the floor and she stood, naked from the waist up. Jennifer's breasts were absolutely gorgeous. It was most likely the thought of ruining their perfection that precluded my succumbing to her wishes and ravishing her ventricles.

"Do it, Mr. Scottie! Heart fuck me!" She wanted me to pump the pump. This struck me as funny. My drug-addled mind vapor locked as it contemplated the sensations likely to accompany a bout of cardiac rape. It was during the ensuing delirium that Jennifer managed to breach the flimsy defenses of my better judgment. I returned to reality to find her kneeling before me, singing into my open fly.

"Rise, oh children, from your sleep. Come play before the Lord," she crooned in lovely mezzo-soprano. The plot had thickened in my momentary absence, and so had my member at the sight of that comely lass prostrate before the serpent's lair. I had to act. I knew if I didn't defuse the ticking timebomb of my own lust, I would likely spend the remainder of my life serving a sentence for murder by unspeakable sodomy. I could hear Jonny arguing before a stone cold jury:

"He never *meant* to spike her pain killers with opium. And pumping her pump...that was an accident too." The presiding judge would, at that point, ask for clarification as to what exactly "pump her pump" meant. Jonny would then show an expensive computer animation of my grizzled dick plunging into a beating, bloody human heart until a glut of digital semen exploded from the intruder, rendering the heart still. His Honor would then dismiss the jury and hand down a summary judgment of, "guilty as charged." An on-the-spot death sentence would be added to the verdict in postscript. I imagine Jonny's eyes growing wide with professional disappointment as the judge pulls his black robe over his head, getting the executioner effect just right, and beats me to death with his gavel. Jonny has me stuffed and files an appeal.

Jennifer had grown increasingly insistent and, despite my horrific visions of the future, I was succumbing.

No rhetoric of Sandra's could have been a more eloquent argument for the existence of God than what happened next. Lying, face up, on the floor, I waited breathlessly for Jennifer to throw herself onto my proffered spike. She swayed above me, her oscillations growing increasingly unstable, until finally she rose onto the balls of her feet and fell forward in earnest. I closed my eyes in anticipation of whatever sensory wonders awaited me on the downside of her fall.

The Nexus of Crisis

The front door burst open and two Jehovah's Witness thugs, operating under Sandra's direction, rushed into the room and caught Jennifer just as she was about to slake her lust. They handled the girl with the ease of fish mongers tossing the day's catch. The darker of the two men snatched up a quilt my aunt had sewn and used it to cover Jennifer's naked torso. He then dragged her across the room, leaving her in Sandra's care, before returning to assist his Caucasoid henchman in kicking the shit out of me—forgiveness and compassion falling by the wayside.

The pair went at me like men possessed. Between Jennifer's suppressed libido and their pent-up aggression, it was becoming increasingly apparent that these people desperately needed to get out more. I was in deep over my head and knew it. The best and only defense I could muster was assuming the fetal position and protecting my face, cock and balls from the kicks and punches the brothers Neanderthal rained down on me. The time of my time had come and gone—I was sure of it…I was going to die.

Blackness descended on me in a welcome wave of impending unconsciousness. I'd resigned myself to a closed casket funeral when, from the corner of a swollen eye, I saw a patch of darkness move across the room with ridiculous speed. There was something strange, familiar yet foreign, about this shadow among the shadows of my failing vision.

A scream, piercing, poignant, and unequivocally mortifying, coincided with the abrupt cessation of the blows.

"Dear Lord God Jesus, protect and preserve us!" I heard Sandra wail over the shriek. A second discernable sound went up from the melee. It was growling—Bro's growling.

Raising my chin from the gore splattered ruin of my shirt, I peered out from between broken fingers and beheld a formerly unimaginable scene. Blood…belching gluts of

93

DOC SOLOMMEN

blood pulsed from behind a hand the wounded linebacker had cupped to his abdomen. The bastard was trying desperately to stem the bleeding flowing from his gut while simultaneously retreating from what had suddenly turned into a very bad scene. Across the room, his associate was struggling with a precarious predicament of his own. Backed against an antique armoire and brandishing a desk lamp, the powerful Negro stood ready to make a last ditch attempt to defend himself against none other than old Bro. The dog I'd written off as a career cripple suddenly appeared criminally insane and dangerous to the extreme that only lunatics, in their immunity from civil and criminal law, can attain. The animal radiated death and a tangible sense of the artistic. I felt his thoughts. He wasn't just going to snuff the militant man of God. He was going to maim him with panaché.

Cracking beneath the hopelessness, the cornered oaf swung the desk lamp in a clumsy, poorly planned arc. The fixture's weight caused it to separate into two utterly useless halves joined together by a length of electric wiring.

Bro seized the opportunity and uncoiled like an electrocuted mongoose. He ran between the thug's legs, executed a bone jarring 180 degree turn and sank his formidable dentition into the soft membranous tissue between the man's ankle and Achilles' tendon. The sound of flesh puncturing was horrible—a grotesque snap sounding like a rock hitting aluminum siding. I watched, transfixed with awe and admiration, as the dog flexed his great shoulders and twisted his head perpendicular to the man's foot. Tendon separated from bone and the once daunting man was laid low. He fell blubbering to one knee. The sight of him genuflecting before his conqueror, an evil, black, demon dog, will remain with me forever.

"Dear God, save your servant!" the fallen Negro sobbed in tones of mortal fear.

He can't help you now, cock meat.

The man's eyes grew wide with unmitigated horror and

he spit up a thin stream of stinking vomit as the realization that the animal had *spoken* dawned upon him. A stain spread across the front of his trousers and the unmistakable reek of feces fouled the air as the dog circled his fallen prey.

Arrogant swine, Bro began. He crossed the room and bristled at Sandra, the delirious Jennifer, and the remaining thug, all of whom stood mute—paralyzed with fear. Crouching, Bro sprang in a lethally graceful movement that carried him the full length of the room. His yawning maw met the crippled man's screaming face with the full force of his seething, canine rage behind it. Fragile bones, the framework of the star-crossed man's sinuses, flaked into utter ruination. Grasping his newly concave face, the Negro staggered into the corner where he collapsed in a bloody, wheezing mass. The animal loped over to where the man sat propped against the expensively papered wall, and casually tore his throat out.

Chapter 11

Backpedal

The ironies inherent with watching a Jehovah's Witness hitman bleed to death at the fangs of a handicapped dog are dangerously close to the upper limit of what an acid-wrecked junkie can handle. I clasped my hands to the sides of my head to keep it from exploding. It is the body's natural tendency, in instances such as these, to turn against and eradicate the offensive or diseased component—in this case the head. I fought for and somehow won control of my faculties. When the throbbing and spasming that had been terrorizing my cranial landscape finally subsided altogether, I began the painful process of assessing the situation and deliberating possible courses of action.

The Negro was dead. Good riddance. His associate had lapsed into mild shock, more from the revolting appearance of his mutilated love handle than any actual loss of blood, I thought. Sandra had retreated to the front porch where she'd fallen to the floor and was writhing around in the throes of some kind of *Lordgasm*. The convulsion would start with Sandra on her back, eyes rolling, hands at her sides, palms down with fingers splayed. She would then arch her back violently, knocking her head against the deck's hardwood planking in the process. Repeated impacts of her head against the teak took their toll on Sandra. After a short series of twisting fits she lay working her jaw in an ongoing silent scream and began thrashing her legs about in grand-mal fashion. So wildly did her extremities flail, that Sandra somersaulted over, landing on her face with brain jarring brutality.

In retrospect, I realize this face-down posture greatly upset the woman. Sobs would wrack her and she would shriek out:

"I can see the beast! I am made to look upon him! Holy Lord Jesus Christ God Jehovah, You are my savior, my captain, my fucking *astronaut*. Deliver me from this evil. Amen!"

With those words, she would writhe with even more ferocity until she flopped, face up, and repeated the cycle. Sandra managed this some half-dozen times before finally whacking her head so violently that she passed out.

Only one of my visitors remained—dear, sweet Jennifer. She was wickedly twisted with drug and seemed to have taken absolutely no notice of the violent, homicidal events that had transpired.

She's kind of cute, isn't she, Scottie? the dog intoned from somewhere behind me.

"Shut up you murderous regression!" I hissed. "How the hell are we going to get ourselves out of this little cluster fuck?"

He flexed his jaws, and the blood caked into the surrounding fur cracked like wet cardboard. Patches of the stuff fell to the floor around him. I was under the impression that the dog was going to say something but instead, he vomited gracelessly. Well into his second or third wretch, Bro's bowels let go and a sinister bluish paste flowed, fouling his rear upholstery. It was then that I noticed the partially digested gel-coats bobbing in the pool of vomit. The speed—the 20/20's. "My god," I marveled. "The suicidal glutton has been into the satchel."

Driven by desperation, I ventured into the dangerous space surrounding the disgorging animal. "How much?" I demanded. "How much did you eat?" The sheer violence of his purge eclipsed the strength of the dog's frail limbs, and he went over like an abandoned bicycle. I watched, helpless, as my beloved nemesis plied the air, his remaining muscular control given over to bizarre running motions that succeeded only in moving his hairy bulk through a series of loops similar to those executed by Sandra a short time earlier. The eruption of blue substance from the animal's rectum continued, unabated, and I was reduced by panic to once again rummaging sloppily through my brain for potential alibis with which to pacify Wilson.

A supreme act of will was required, but I forced myself back to the unfurling disaster and resumed my perfunctory interrogation. "How much did you eat? How much and what kinds of poisons have you ingested, you injudicious prick?" I demanded. Grasping him by the ears, I peered intently into the dog's almond eyes and saw the terror coalescing therein.

Slowly, painfully, Bro righted himself and lurched, bouncing off walls and furniture, toward the pantry. Intuition told me he wanted ingress so I opened the door for him. Slobbering fabulously, he immersed himself haunch deep into my oubliette of cleanliness. When Bro finally pulled himself from the pantry, he had clasped in his jaws a box of ALL laundry detergent. Understanding dawned on me like a blow to the head; he'd eaten everything in the satchel—ALL of it.

Our eyes met a second time. The fear was being driven from his gaze, replaced by a stern look of singular purpose. He would *not* die inadvertently and without flair. No, the dog was the master of his own destiny. Piss on anyone who believed otherwise. He was going to die, that much was certain, but he would do so on his own terms. *Don't interfere.* That was the silent implication conveyed by the prolonged stare in which he held me. Feeling I understood, the brave beast stuffed his muzzle deep into the box of detergent and commenced his last supper.

I felt the presence of the unwitting spectators, living and dead, behind me. We watched together as he devoured the entire damnable box, anionic surfactants and all.

A tense moment passed between the dog's pulling his detergent flecked head from the box of poison and his crumpling to a disorganized heap. I was beyond grief. Bobbing, numb and stupid to my record collection, I fished out Pink Floyd's, *The Wall.* I listened to the record for three straight days, never once moving from my lounge chair.

Chapter 12

Downtime

On the morning of the third day, the telephone exploded to life, shattering the vigil I'd kept for 72, miserable hours. I answered it on the sixth ring and winced as the forgotten hostility of the outside world pumped like black bile into my right ear.

"Scottie…Scottie…are you there? Talk to me, you fucking hermit." It was Jonny.

"Jonny," I whispered. "Bro's dead."

"Oh, Scottie, you sound like shit. Did I understand that last thing? Bro's dead? Not like, you're going to kill him because he pissed you off again, but clinically, irreversibly croaked?"

"Yes, he's dead. The crazy bastard overdosed on laundry detergent."

"Christ, there are those among us who just don't know when to stop," he offered—callow attorney's sympathy.

"There's, more," I croaked.

Jonny picked up on my crisis vibe immediately. He could smell the legal discord through 15 miles of telephone cable. "I'll be there in half an hour." The line went dead.

Chapter 13

Formulation and Forensics

Jonny arrived shortly after one on the rainy afternoon of November 26th. He let himself in and staggered just a little as he rounded the corner separating foyer from living room. The throat torn corpse in the corner was well into its decomposition. The reek, judging by Jonny's reaction, must have been remarkable. I'd been in such close proximity to the macabre heap the past days that I'd acclimated to its malodorousness. The other thug had bled to death just inside the front door. It seemed his wound was more serious than I'd initially perceived.

Just after sunrise on the second day, Sandra had awakened from her self-induced concussion convinced that she was Mother Theresa. I vaguely recall her dragging both the dead thug and the clinically psychotic Jennifer out the door and up the street. I read in the paper some days later that she was picked up by a county sheriff's deputy who, upon noting the states of her companions, booked her on suspicion of drug trafficking and murder. Alas, poor Sandra refused to unclasp her hands from prayer when the officer attempted to cuff her. This constituted resisting arrest and the lawman was duty bound to club her into submission with his baton, then secure the cuffs and unceremoniously deposit her into his cruiser. I imagine Sandra sitting, tall and proud, in the Crown Victoria's plastic rear seat, singing a medley of hymns, until an ambulance and coroner's van arrived for her comrades. To this day, I cannot fathom why she chose to leave the Negro's grizzled corpse behind. The fact that she dragged his sidekick away dismisses arguments of necrophobia. Perhaps she planned to return for him after seeing Jennifer and the first cadaver to wherever it was she'd been taking them. I suppose no one will ever know.

I was grateful for Jonny's presence. His line of work made him the perfect man to manage the dicey situation at hand. He began damage control by phoning his office and instructing Helen to clear his appointment schedule. He explained to her that he was supervising his mother's exhumation and would be back behind the desk in a day or two.

"Go upstairs and take a shower. You smell like shit," he ordered me.

I responded mechanically to his command. Without a word, I rose and made for my upstairs bathroom. Forty minutes later, I emerged feeling nearly human. Jonny instructed me to play loud music, check my mail, hit some golf balls over the embankment in my back yard—in a word, normal type things. It was imperative, he explained, that I be seen by my neighbors. He had driven my Cadillac over and parked it in plain sight—the Lotus locked securely away in the garage. No one would know Jonny was present and that's just how he wanted it.

While I was out fucking around on the property, Jonny used my expensive set of Chicago Cutlery to dismember the Negro's rotting corpse and stuff the pieces into one gallon freezer bags. It took him the better part of the afternoon to properly package the bloody mess. When he reached the head, Jonny was forced to explore more elaborate means of disposal. After some thought and a period of unmentionable trial and error, he settled on a course of action.

Using a pair of vice grips, he removed the thug's teeth from their sockets. The shoddy dentistry complete, Jonny stuffed the man's penis (which he'd severed with a paring knife and set aside specifically for this purpose) into the toothless mouth, then forced the ugly aperture closed. In the unlikely event the body was ever found, Jonny wanted its condition to suggest a premeditated, vengeance killing, not the random act of a lunatic dog.

Next, my illustrious attorney went downstairs, opened the access panel at the base of my hot water heater and blew out the pilot light. He held his hand over the opening for about twenty seconds, allowing natural gas to accumulate in concentration. The madman then produced his lighter, sparked the flint and dove for cover. The ensuing explosion was small, controlled to the point that I, working with my pitching wedge not 15 yards away, mistook it for an article of furniture being moved. The blast was, however, sufficiently powerful to completely destroy the water heater's innards. Returning to the living room, Jonny spent the next 90 minutes meticulously removing every fiber and drop of blood evincing recent events.

I'd made real progress toward bettering my short game when Jonny called me inside to a lunch of my own cold cuts and champagne. Upon inspecting the living room, I was absolutely astounded by the impeccable condition to which he'd restored it. When we finished lunch, Jonny instructed me to call a plumber he'd selected at random from the Yellow Pages, and have the individual come out to investigate the cause of my sudden hot water deficit.

7:15 p.m. Pacific standard time: A shifty looking fellow, probably a former suit salesman, pulled up outside the main house in a van emblazoned with the *conceived-on-lunch-hour* logo of the Manjo Plumbing Company. The business's directory advertisement had read, "Don't trust your plumbing to any Joe. Insist on Manjo." Manjo Plumbing had not been Jonny's first choice, but it was the only provider of pipe fitting services receptive to the idea of 7:00 p.m. house calls.

The name patch identified the plumber as Monty. Carrying out Jonny's instructions to a tee, I described to Monty, who nodded repeatedly and chewed his gum with a fervor that suggested he wasn't at all listening to what I was saying, the specific nature of my plumbing woes.

"It just crapped out," I lamented. "Everything seemed fine this morning when I showered, but then, around 2:30 or 3:00, I tried topping off the Jacuzzi and couldn't get any hot water. I tried every faucet in the place and got only ice fucking cold water for my trouble."

"Did you check the water heater, sir?" Monty inquired, the lusty look of realized potential revenue playing across his shifty features.

"The water heater?" I inquired.

"Yeah," Monty hastened. "It's a big round thing that heats water for the house."

"Oh, I know what you're talking about," I beamed with mock stupidity. "It's by the furnace. Follow me." I led Monty downstairs and stood by, feigning amazement as he sniffed the furnace room air. As he did so, glimmers of fear flickered across his face.

"My God!" he exclaimed. "Don't you smell the gas?"

"Now that you mention it, I do smell something," I conceded, still following Jonny's orders to the letter. "Let me turn the light on and maybe…"

"No! No! For christsake, whatever you do, *don't* do that!" Monty implored as he turned on a heel and ran from the small room. I smiled to myself and followed him into the hall. He spent a full five minutes explaining the perils of natural gas leaks and admonishing me for what he described as "suicidal behavior." Monty then suggested I go upstairs while he went outside and disabled the flow of gas at the main. It took him about 15 minutes to locate the valve and close it. Thinking the house still too hazardous, he insisted we wait outside an additional 15 minutes.

When we finally returned to the furnace room, Monty examined the water heater and let loose a whistle of disbelief. Signs of physical delirium shook him as Monty explained to me how the pilot light had most likely gone out, allowing the appliance to fill with gas. He proceeded to explain the intricacies of a supposedly failsafe system that had been engineered into the water heater. This consisted of cryptic gadgetry that was supposed to electronically re-ignited the pilot light should it go out. It was Monty's opinion that this failsafe system failed utterly, and sufficient gas had collected in the ill-fated water heater to blow it up.

"I can have one out here by nine tomorrow morning. That puts you back in hot water by noon, Mr. Scirocco," Monty informed me as he perused his date book. I recognized his schedule checking for the bullshit it was. The crook was trying to pressure me into signing on the dotted line with the implication that he was terribly in demand. I wanted to tell him to fuck himself, but I knew Jonny's plan wouldn't tolerate it. I'd no choice but to continue along my preordained course.

"That's not acceptable, Monty," I growled. "I'll be goddamned if I'm going to stay here, living like an Amazon basin savage while my neighbors wallow in their Jacuzzis and hot showers. I want a new water heater here and installed by midnight tonight. I don't give a rat's ass what it costs. Do you understand me, Mister?"

An ecstasy of greed descended over the man. He drooled unconsciously as he phoned a number of warehouses trying to find my replacement water heater.

At 1:00 a.m., I wrote Monty a check for $3,200 and threw him out of my house. He offered to cart the old, burnt out water heater to the dump but I declined, explaining how it would make an excellent barbecue grill. He agreed enthusiastically, as boot-lickers are prone to do, and drove off—probably to the local pub.

Jonny emerged from hiding, patted me on the back and sent me off to bed. I was happy to go.

Chapter 14

Tasty Paste, Tangy Bonanza

While I was sleeping off a compressed lifetime's worth of stress and poison, Jonny filled the old water heater with the freezer bags containing the deceased. He'd taken the teeth he extracted and ground them into a chalky pulp that he baked into an enormous batch of truly horrible chocolate chip cookies.

Before the sun had risen, Jonny accomplished the twofold task of anonymously dropping the cookies into a dry goods collection bin at a cross town food bank, and burying the water heater adjacent my driveway. We spent the day leveling earth, constructing forms and mixing the concrete that gave rise to the exquisite basketball court I own, but have yet to use.

Crisis had been averted thanks to Jonny's quick thinking and ruthless nature. I will never forget the debt of gratitude I owe him for that. At the time, I tried stammering some lame expression of thanks, but Jonny stopped me before I humiliated myself. Clasping his hand to my shoulder, he smiled and shook his head. My attorney departed in a squeal of tires that proclaimed his joy at being reunited with his Lotus.

The silence that followed Jonny's spirited exit drove

home the unattractive truth. Bro was gone. Jonny had, in his necessary haste to address more pressing matters, packed the dog into a 33 gallon garbage bag and deposited the oozing mess on the back porch where it had laid rotting with zeal. Mustering my courage, I made my way toward dog's final resting place. Propelled by a powerful sense of duty, I approached and began to carefully lay back Bro's crude burial shroud. What I found interred in the garbage bag filled me with such a mix of revulsion and macabre fascination as I shall never forget. The twisted mess of arthritis degenerated bones remained, more or less, intact. The flesh, indeed all of the soft tissue had, however, undergone a radical metamorphosis. Instead of muscle, sinew, blood, and assorted organs, only blue paste remained. This strange substance had the approximate color and consistency of toothpaste and smelled not of decay, but of antiseptic cleanliness.

I had known and loved the dog. This perhaps explains my next actions: Squatting at the edge of the blue puddle, I inserted the index finger of my right hand into the mess. I raised the finger to my face and closely examined the adhering residue. I smelled it. This proved inconclusive so, following some bizarre sense of logic, I tasted it.

My body stiffened and I fell flat to the decking. There was a fleeting vision of Sandra dashing herself senseless (how long ago had that been) and then, pure madness. I suffered the indignity of incontinence as my physical body divorced itself from my control. The light went dim as my pupils dilated to the size of quarters and then…I traveled the astral plane. The sky above turned from gray to the powder blue of the magic paste I'd ingested. A colossal zipper appeared, replacing the sun. The zipper fell, splitting asunder the two halves of the sky. Out from the rent in the heavens emerged a stupendously enormous penis. It floated out into the afternoon like the resurrected Hindenburg. Attached to its sides were a number of propulsive engines that

enhanced both the monolith's mobility and its uncanny resemblance to the fiery dirigible of old. The engines surged to life and the horror uncoiled, swinging its great head pendulously to and fro and snatching up and swallowing entire airliners and flocks of migrating geese. It sucked lightning from thunderstorms, causing the dark silhouettes of its moon sized testicles to glow with electrical infusion. Mylar balloons, Sears catalogs, and Motown 8-tracks shot from the floating phallus as it continued its trek across the sky. Flannel couches and clowns dotted the emission as well.

A host of misshapen angels fluttered out from the heavenly fly and took up formation around the great prick. These were unlike any cherubim or seraphim of Biblical account. Gray and mottled were they—diseased, and pitiful to behold. Most were without legs and had in their stead a gaggle of twisted buds, each of which had at its tip a twitching sphincter. The ghastly apertures opened at random and disgorged flies, lungfish, tapeworms and occasionally the bleating of goats into the pristine air. The company of angels proved to be a choir, albeit a bad one. Having organized themselves, they began shrieking and cursing in all of the world's languages. Their horrible discord culminated in what sounded like a mortified Julio Iglesias trying to remove a hot nail from his foot while floating in a sewer.

Five verses into what was beginning to look like a very lengthy oratorio, the choir seemed to lose interest and, a few at a time, began fluttering back into the great, heavenly fly.

As the last unwholesome angel disappeared from sight, a figure appeared and could be seen making its way forward along the length of the flying phallus. As it drew near, my heart leapt in my chest. It was Bro, and he looked magnificent. A bright light shone around his head and following submissively behind him was a pack of exquisite bitches. These were of every conceivable breed and howled out Bro's praises. Occasionally, one would snarl menacingly at a rival as they vied for opportunities to lick and groom his revitalized haunches. The caravan of divinity advanced until Bro stood, superb in the splendor of his godhead, at the ridge that delineated the head of the great swaying genital.

Scottie, you look like shit, man, he began, sounding no different than he had in life. *I have to tell you,* he continued. *As fan-fucking-tastic as it is up here—you know, perfect health, unbelievable virility and limitless female companionship, not to mention access to these over the top theatrics—I'm going to miss you, old boy.*

I tried to speak but the nerves between my brain and mouth were misfiring. All I could manage was a series of mandibular spasms and a little drool.

Save your strength, Scottie. I know what's in that stuff you accidentally ate. Be advised, my friend. That blue paste is a concentrated hybrid of each and every one of those spiffy pharmaceuticals you had in that satchel of yours. In my last terrestrial moment, I was under the impression that the drugs must have somehow interacted with all of the residual arthritis medicine floating around my system. Now that I'm dead, though, I can tell you what really happened. It seems, my friend, that unrealized potential collects as an actual physical substance in the bloodstream. Whether through apathy, stupidity, shortsightedness or, as in my case, physiological handicap, the stuff builds up until it reaches toxic levels. Once toxicity is achieved, the brain implodes on itself. Not an overt, medically detectable implosion, but a subtle series of short circuits and flame-outs, the combined effects of which are manifested in any number of criminal behaviors. Now, don't get me wrong, Scottie. I'm not comparing my homicidal lapse to the sloppy, left field antics of wanton butchers like Gacy or Dahmer. Christ, those guys were sick—fucked in the head. I doubt they perceived any potential in themselves at all. I'm talking about passions and drives that exceed the scope of human restraint. I'm talking about Van Gogh's ear. I'm talking about the art of Giger or the writings of Burroughs. I'm

talking about Keith Moon, John Bonham and Jimi Hendrix. I'm talking about Bon fucking Scott, man! All of them gone to great and glorious martyrdoms at the merciless hands of their individual passions. He paused to regain his composure. The dog was whipping himself into an afterlife frenzy.

Christ, Scottie, I almost shit myself, he confessed. At the mention of offal, the bitch grooming Bro's nether reaches bared her teeth and warded off her sisters, all of whose ears had perked up at the idea of cleansing their shit-fouled master. The outburst was, however, brief. An uneasy order settled over the assembly and Bro resumed his discourse.

I was a victim of my own innate magnificence—too out of sync with a world that just wasn't ready for me—a stranger in a lame land. It's really much better this way, Scottie. Death becomes me.

Okay, enough of that shit. I'm here for two reasons. Firstly, it's my responsibility to see to it that you don't spend the rest of your life carrying around a head full of guilt about my passing. We both know you were only trying to alleviate my suffering. Hell, Scottie, for the most part it was working. It isn't your fault that my inner demons drove me to dredge that bag of drugs like a pie tin full of giblets. I wanted to do it, man! Look back over the course of our association. Did I ever do anything I didn't want to do?

I began to feel better as I considered the question. It was true, the dog never had done anything he truly didn't want to do. He had been, and apparently remained the master of his destiny.

The second item on the agenda is your salvation.

I reeled in revulsion. What was he saying? Bro had spoken the words that were, in my estimation, the stigma of stigmas. He might as well have discussed diet plans with the Carpenter family, or ski vacations with the Bonos. The beast sensed my outrage, though, and his responding laughter peeled like thunder through the azure sky.

Calm down, jackass, he boomed. *I'm not talking about*

the salvation of your immortal soul. Take it from someone who knows first-hand, that's all bullshit. What I refer to when I say 'salvation' is your increased financial stature. It's time you realized your potential. We both know you're a shitty restaurateur. Hell, if it wasn't for Jonny the whole game would have been over six months after kickoff and you would be jerking off into the scratchy woolen sheets at The Bread of Life mission.

Deep inside, I knew it was true. I was a beneficiary of favorable circumstances. It *had* always struck me as strange that I was looked to as a captain of industry when in actuality, I was little more than the heavy breasted figurehead carved onto the prow of the Scirocco Taco ship. Bro was right. I desperately needed a groovier gig.

Yes you do, old boy. A groovier gig, indeed, a gig in which every meal is a banquet and every party a shindig. The deceased apparently read minds. This was very disconcerting.

You're going to regain control of your sympathetic nervous system in about three minutes, Scottie, so listen, the dog intoned. *The blue paste is the answer to your career dilemma. Collect it and get it to Wilson. It's the purest, most unadulterated poison ever to seep up from the primordial bowel. The amount you ingested was enough to string out and very likely kill every man, woman, child, and reborn Christian in North Carolina. You're only alive because I have some jurisdiction in these matters. One one-thousandth of one gram of that blue shit is potent enough to keep a grown man crazy for forty-eight hours. Nothing like it has ever existed. Get it to Wilson and have him move it through his channels. There's about twenty-five kilograms of paste lying beside you in my body bag. It will easily fetch a thousand dollars a gram from Wilson's upscale junkies. Do the math, Scottie. That's about twenty-five-million in tax free, U.S. dollars. Think about it, man. A way out of the legitimate, but let's face it, boring restaurant business. I'll see*

*you in forty-six years and sixty-one days. Shit! I wasn't sup-
posed to tell you that. Oh well. Until then.*

He turned and began making his way back down the
cosmic cock. As he disappeared from sight, I heard the
echoes of his last words ricocheting across the sky.

Do the math, Scottie. Do the math.

And then, he was gone.

The vision faded like soft porn from a blown Trinitron.
Slowly, mercilessly, the sky regained its characteristic
shade of somber November. A cold rain had fallen during
my fantastic, paranormal experience, and the first discernable feeling to creep up the mending neural pathways of my
spinal cord was numbing, deathly cold.

I gathered the corners of Bro's shroud together and
dragged it and myself into the house and its promise of
warmth. When feeling returned to my hands, I called
Wilson. I didn't know whether the shaking in my fingers
was a lingering effect of exposure or the first physical
symptom of genuine happiness.

Chapter 1

Sacraments and Incriminations

T he cavernous expanse of pews, pathways, shrines and statues, all girded by the somber stations of the cross, echoed pitifully with the dainty blowing of an old woman's nose and then the slamming of doors behind her as she took her leave of St. James Cathedral. Matt was alone, in a manner of speaking. The silence that ensued the elderly woman's exodus roared up in his skull and sent his gaze moving nervously from the condemningly serene face of the Blessed Virgin to the tortured and contorted visage of her son, who hung on a great cross above and at the rear of the sprawling altar. Dust and the curling blue smoke of incense rose and writhed in the kaleidoscope of multi-colored bolts issued from a stupifyingly enormous stained glass window. The colored lights met and mingled on the altar in such a way that one would have expected the crucified Christ to descend from the unpleasantness of the recreation of his passion and do the Hustle. The somber deity did not, however, disco, and Matt's flight of fantasy crashed with Libyan vigor into the churning sea of madness which was becoming his reality.

The confessional's ancient door creaked on arthritic hinges as Matt, momentarily blind in the mildewy darkness, knelt and began the recitation of repentance. "Bless me Father, for I've sinned. It's been..." *How long had it been?* "It's been about twelve years since my last confession. These are my sins." On the opposite side of the opaque screen separating the confessional from the small vestibule in which the presiding priest dispensed admonition, Father Vivian was acutely aware of the fact that the young man's voice had suddenly changed—become more shrill and maniacal, his train of thought more disjointed and largely vulgar. "I stole a puppy because I thought it was cute!" the voice blurted out. "I dropped it into a grass-catcher bag my grandfather had hanging in his garage so no one would find it. I threw it handfuls of dog food and let it live in its own shit and piss in a sweltering hot garage during a murderously torrid summer. Its incessant yelping began to smack of ingratitude though, and I had to beat it with a welding rod and unceremoniously drop it back into the bag where one day I found it, shit-matted and stinking, teetering on the brink of death. I returned the wretch, with which I had become entirely disenchanted, to the same yard from which I had wrested it and washed my hands of the matter of its fate."

Silence—Father Vivian, sensing it was time to commence with the dispensing of forgiveness, began his tired monologue and was rudely cut off.

"I've killed frogs and snakes by the hundreds. I've shot them with BB guns, impaled them on sharpened sticks, burned them with gasoline and cut them with razors. If it was available, I poured bleach into the rents I'd opened in the scaly flesh and delighted in the animal's undiluted agony. I've killed birds with pellets and poisons. I've even crucified them on crosses made of wood scraps. One I wounded with a poorly placed pellet and nailed, still screaming and bubbling blood, to a cross that I set afloat in the filth of the little Calumet River and watched till it disappeared from sight on the carcinogenic currents. I tried to decapitate a six-toed kitten, but my resolve waned at the last second. The resulting errant blow succeeded only in severing a tiny foreleg, the stump of which shot twin streams of bright arterial blood across my parents' basement floor. The animal's mouth stretched and shivered in a grotesque silent scream that went on and on, even as the head lolled across the blood-slicked concrete. I put a small dog in a footlocker and then riddled the box from close range with .357 ordinance. I ran a friend's pet white rat through a table saw and cleverly posed the front half so it appeared that the rodent was emerging from the overturned shoebox that was its home."

Vivian was growing nervous.

"I tried to coerce a guinea pig into performing fellatio. It bit my penis so I had no choice but to duct-tape the offending animal to a skateboard which I propelled at (quite literally) breakneck speeds into a basement wall until its protesting passenger expired in a jackpot of pissing and pellet-shaped turds. I sprained my hand delivering a robust upper-cut to the head of a startled steer which I'd lured to myself with a handful of grass shoots."

"My son…" Vivian interjected

"I'm not finished!" came the snarling reply from the intensifying darkness opposite the suddenly brittle and insubstantial seeming textile partition separating cleric from confessor.

"I've reveled in bloodying the eyes and noses of those I call 'Friend.' I have hanged one such friend by the flesh of his back from the jutting points atop a chain-link fence and took my casual leave of him and his agonized screams and sobbing pleas for assistance. I have raged and cursed God in the blind fury of youth's frustration and arrogant indignance. I have slashed tires, left side front and rear mind you, so the victim of my attention was left without even a salvageable pair and had no choice but to replace the set in its entirety. All of this in retaliation for a passing but unappreciated remark he had made regarding my character.

I have engaged in every conceivable manner of sexual depravity and bear the scars of disease as trophies. I have reveled in the defloration of virgins and the debasing of the virtuous. The maiden's cry of momentary anguish and the adulteress's gasp of shocked exhilaration have played like the sweetest melodies in my jaded ears. I have inspired the chaste to submit to acts of sodomy for which names do not exist and thrilled to their begrudging, guilt-ridden climaxes and the hot effusions of remorse that followed. I have implied love and delivered only semen in its stead. When sued for explanations for my inevitable desertions I have been brutal in my admonitions and quick to express my own exasperation at my victims' impertinence and ingratitude. I have taken particular delight in the tempting of the righteous with pleasures both carnal and chemical and have considered their lunatic detours from the path of spiritual fortitude my greatest successes. On one occasion I coerced a close friend, who struggled mightily in the name of his savior against the dark side of his nature, into an establishment of dubious repute wherein young women, passive to the point of apparent delirium, displayed surgically augmented attributes with a frankness that would have moved a gynecologist to reminiscences of medical school. How well I recall the epic battle between physiological drive and ecclesiastical dogma that played across his features in a rush of sidelong glances and incoherent mutterings. How I reveled in my achievement as we stepped together, after physiology's inevitable victory was won, into the seedy half-light of the carnal house with my assurance of 'You're going to love it' echoing in our collective consciousness."

 Father Vivian had, in his mounting horror, moved with the calculated stealth of a cur toward the vestibule door and deliverance from the foulness of the creature in his confessional when the thing made known to him its paramount transgression.

"And I killed the one I love."

Chapter 2

Dozing for Dollars

The sound of bleating erupted from the forward cargo bin as 178 terrified sheep, all screaming and shitting one another, simultaneously protested the application of takeoff power. "Torque set. Airspeed alive. V1." The first officer gave the customary call outs as the aircraft and its unenthusiastic cargo bolted down Boeing Field's runway 31 left. Ed, the captain, noted, with no small satisfaction, that thus far everything had progressed according to plan. Prevailing winds dictated a northerly takeoff, which would accommodate the expeditious completion of the night's mission.

"Rotate," the first officer's words derailed Ed's train of thought. Referencing the airspeed indicator, Ed applied back pressure and the majestic machine rose up from the ground. The aircraft lurched aggressively forward as its wheels left the ground and clawed at the air in a mad campaign to sate its gluttonous appetite for speed and altitude. The smell of shit and the raucous bleating reached a crescendo as the landing gear slammed into the wells.

"After takeoff checks," Ed intoned.

"Gear up, lights off, yaw damper on, prop sync on, climb power set, fuel caps secure, pressurization check. Looks like she's gonna fly, captain," the first officer confidently replied.

"Good boy, Jonny. Now fetch me a cup of coffee like a good lad." Ed was possessed of the unique and fascinating ability to speak without ever compromising the sly smile that hung like a drunken crescent moon beneath his hoary mustache.

"Why me? Why am I always getting the coffee?" Jonny protested.

"What do you think the 'co' in 'copilot' stands for?" Ed's smile waxed to its gibbous stage. "Calm the cargo while you're at it, will you, Jonny."

Coffee-pilot Jonny reached into the recesses behind his seat and produced a wicked looking aluminum bat. The crew compartment door closed with a "snick" as he disappeared into the bowels of the fuselage whistling John Fogerty's "Centerfield."

Chapter 3

Travis

Travis had a plan. He fancied it a good one. All winter long he had pumped and preened in the weight room. His narcissistic fervor bore firm fruit. A subsequent trip to the local department store provided the props his grand design would require if it was to prove successful.

The first light of that summer morning peeked over the Cascade Mountains to find Travis negotiating the deserted streets of West Seattle. He made his slow, predatory way to Alkia Beach, a popular spot among Seattleites searching for that certain special someone. Parking was not a problem, given the early hour, and Travis pulled his stylish, sport pick-up into one of the coveted, beachside parking spaces. He spent a few moments oiling his body with water resistant sunscreen before wading into the shallow water. Then, armed with a snorkel, a toy periscope and a pitchfork (which he had, through skillful filing, made to reasonably resemble a trident) he set his strange plan in motion. Squatting in some four feet of water, snorkel and periscope deployed, Travis waited patiently for the crowds.

Chapter 4

Matt

Matt had a trampoline in his backyard. He also had a girlfriend, rightly named "Lillyanne" but commonly referred to as "Fred." Matt and Fred loved nothing better than to leap, up and down, on the trampoline while engaged in a sporadically airborne game of "Touchy-Feely." So great was their fervor one summer evening that, on the downside of a particularly spirited leap, they did, indeed, miss the trampoline entirely and collide violently with the ground. Alas, poor Fred was killed instantly when the majority of her reproductive organs left her body with Matt's right hand which, along with the rest of him, bounced after the initial, face down, impact and came to rest some 30 feet from her. For his own part, Matt's rigid penis, upon striking the Earth, had snapped smartly in the middle, giving new meaning to the "Painful erection" cliché. Which brings to mind...

> *There was once*
> *a young man from Kent*
> *whose prick was so long*
> *that it bent.*
> *To spare himself trouble*
> *He'd fold it in double*
> *and instead of coming...he went.*

The paramedics arrived and, after adorning Fred in a striking zip-up plastic bag—which matched perfectly the purple and black bruises forming about her ribcage—splinted Matt's penis, sedated him and whisked him off via medivac helicopter to Harborview Hospital.

Chapter 5

Woolite by Moonlight

"**D**o ordain and establish organized prostitution at subsidized rates in Antarctica."

Finishing with a flourish of his arms, Jonny knocked his coffee cup out of its conveniently located holder, precipitating an electrical short-out of the autopilot. A torrent of sheep excrement seeped out of the cargo bay and moved in leisurely ripples up and down the aisle as the aircraft reacted to the malfunction. Ed's coffee remained, thankfully, undisturbed.

"You realize we have to hand fly now," Ed scolded as Jonny jabbed aimlessly at the sizzling autopilot panel.

"Yeah, yeah, yeah, sorry, boss," came the first officer's distracted reply. They both shrugged, having forgotten the aft cargo door controls shared an electrical bus with the autopilot circuits; as the aircraft assumed an uncommanded, nose up attitude, the great doors opened and some two dozen sheep somersaulted out into the cool night air.

"Aw shit," Ed mourned, his smile undiminished. "Can we close those manually, Jonny?"

"Yeah, I think so. I'll have to go back there though," Jonny tensely answered.

"Go then, man. For the Christ's sake, go. Those animals haven't been sheared. The static charge resulting from that much wool being blown around could conceivably…"

But it was too late.

The following morning, the *Post Intelligencer* reported an inexplicable bolt of lightning having issued from a cloudless sky and struck Harborview Hospital. The anomaly caused a building wide power failure. Even the backup generators shorted and caught fire. Forty-one people in the intensive care unit died instantly. The remainder of the patients perished in the ensuing blaze. Those convalescing in the burn unit thought the whole incident a terrific irony.

Chapter 6

Matt Again

The Sikorski S-76 medivac helicopter made a 180-degree turn and proceeded directly to Maddigan Army Hospital on Fort Lewis. Dispatch reported minor trouble with the heli-pad at Harborview.

Chapter 7

Neptune

Emily planned to meet her girlfriends at the beach around noon. Catching the optimal tanning rays was of the utmost importance. For reasons beyond her comprehension, however, she was unable to sleep late that morning. The arduous tasks of showering, shaving, blow drying, making up and dressing were ineffective at dissipating the pent-up energy she was feeling. At 9:00, unable to bear the confines of her apartment any longer, she set out for Alkia Beach. She arrived there at quarter to 10 and congratulated herself for making what had proved an excellent decision. The beach drive was deserted, save a solitary, white sport pick-up truck. Beyond, the mist was only just beginning to lift from the water's surface. Gulls' cries echoed across Puget Sound as the birds traversed the narrow band of clear air between ocean and overcast.

With a deliberateness of fluid motion, for the most part unknown beyond the confines of X-rated movie houses, she tore away her tank top and shorts, adjusted her "new for the season" bathing suit and made her way across the cool sand to the water's edge. The feel of the frigid salt-water on her small feet dashed any thoughts of a morning swim. She was, for the moment, content to stand, arms crossed, at the uppermost reach of the waves and look across the water at the sleeping city.

Some 30 feet out in the shallows a head suddenly appeared. Muscular shoulders and a broad chest followed as who she assumed must be Neptune (or perhaps Poseidon—she never could keep her mythologies straight) rose from the depths of his kingdom. A fearsome trident jutted from one of his strong hands, while in the other he held what appeared to be a snorkel and toy periscope. Emily swooned. She did, however, manage to fall desperately in love (lust) with Neptune (Poseidon) just before consciousness left her. All the while a plume of black smoke continued rising south of the city.

Chapter 8

Endowment

A circle of nurses stared in reverence. The prognosis was not what one would categorize as "good," yet it was not altogether bad. It really came down, as most things do, to one's point of view. Matt was for the most part unharmed. He had incurred some bruised ribs and a mildly sprained ankle, nothing to be considered particularly traumatic. He had, however, also sustained a rather unique injury to his penis, which would, if the urologist's hypothesis was borne out, leave it swollen some three times its normal size for the rest of Matt's life.

Matt was still sedated. The low blood pressure reading displayed on the monitor above his bed had been attributed to his circulatory system's inability to provide his newly expanded genital the blood supply it required. A transfusion had been scheduled for later that morning. In the meantime, a troop of psychologists endeavored to decide on an appropriate course of what would, no doubt, be an extensive program of socio-sexual rehabilitation.

The nurses continued their vigil well into the night. No one was present in the wee morning hours to witness the drawing of the curtain around Matt's bed and the unusual requisition put out for no fewer than six institutional sized tubes of KY Jelly, 17 yards of surgical tubing, a box of sterile rubber gloves, two disposable plastic speculum, a stirrup-equipped birthing table, four high colonic enema bags, one dozen bed pans, a portable defibrillator and six sets of scrubs, one in men's size, five in women's.

Matt was discharged the following morning with no apparent need of counseling. Five I.C.U. nurses had, in the meantime, been admitted to female medicine with uterine displacement. Insurance company statistics would show a short-term rise in such occurrences all through the Puget Sound region.

Chapter 9

Electro-Nostalgia

A s Jonny understood it, voltage hurt and amperage killed. Insomuch as he would eventually wake up, blissfully alive and not in any serious pain, he concluded that static electricity fell somewhere between pain and death, and landed squarely on delusion—a kind of "vamperage." He had a lucid dream.

Hitler and Goëring were throwing darts in a Polish pub. On the ancient dart board hung a gurgling, bloated balloon. Goëring scored a hit. The balloon, filled with Mengele's semen, exploded, sending its contents cascading merrily down the dirty wall. A cockroach's attention was torn from the beer nut it was endeavoring to impregnate by the sound of an explosion high above. The insect turned, attempting to ascertain the cause of the disturbance. Before evolution's masterpiece had a chance to scurry away, however, the milky mess descended upon and drowned it. The corpse twitched once, then twice and perhaps even a third time before convulsing violently and splitting into two, four and finally eight dead cockroaches. Hitler was thrilled and cheered wildly. He vaulted from his chair, slammed the heels of his beautifully polished jack boots together, extended his right arm in a bone-jarring salute and ordered drinks for the entire pub.

Rommell disemboweled a young barmaid with a steak knife and frantically searched her abdominal cavity for Jesse Owens trading cards. Himmler abducted a screaming child from her horrified parents and commenced to strip her. The girl's mother howled in protest. One look from Himmler silenced the woman, though. The child offered no resistance as she was lifted onto a table. Her thin legs were bound at the ankles and pulled behind her head. She began to wail, the pain of having her limbs so severely contorted more than she could bear.

The sound grated on Hitler's nerves. He motioned to a pair of SS guards stationed at the door. The larger of the two left his post, rifle in hand. He approached the table where Himmler was performing and smashed the girl's hips with the butt of his weapon. Again and again he struck the fragile child until her joints were so thoroughly shattered that they forfeited all resistance and her legs not only fell behind her neck, but dangled freely about the middle of her back. Her screams were exquisite; a sound much too wonderful to have come from such a skinny, insubstantial child. Feverish Nazis cursed and elbowed each other as they vied for better views of the proceedings.

Himmler opened his handsome uniform breeches and produced a cock of amazing girth—not unusually lengthy, but wonderfully fat. He stuffed his champion into a porcelain beer stein and began pumping like a Bavarian stallion. His prick flowered into magnificent turgidity. The stein with which he so enthusiastically copulated exploded with a merry *pop* as the dimensions of his gland exceed its capacity. All was in readiness. The tethered child was just regaining consciousness when Himmler rudely mounted and savagely sodomized her. Poor child, her mouth opened but no melodic screams emitted there from. In one glorious instant, faster than the eye could follow, Himmler's onslaught split the girl, perfectly, in half. The two halves, each using the one good arm at its disposal, dragged themselves out of the bar muttering about the exorbitant cover charge and lack of live music. Himmler acknowledged the raucous applause, called for more pretzels and bowed to his führer.

The excitement was more than Hitler could bear. He too would perform. Upon realizing that their beloved dictator intended to grace them with his own, undoubtedly wonderful performance, the crowd all but swooned in lusty anticipation. Even the subtle sound of breathing lulled as the house lights dimmed. A woman, despite her laudable efforts to the contrary, groaned in orgasm as Hitler ascended the stage stairs. Two Aryan lads, fierce, blue eyes ablaze in patriotic fervor, appeared in the wings to attend their messiah. Taking his place at center stage, the führer struck a dramatic pose—arms outstretched, head thrown back in enigmatic contemplation. After a drawn-out moment, his attendants moved silently forward and stripped Hitler of his boots, breeches, jacket, and innumerable military decorations. Tattoos adorned his body: Swastikas with phallic tips, skeletons perched on toilets resembling North African mosques, starving Poles lying prostrate before a beautifully muscled Aryan youth who fed them dog shit and hair. Such were the depictions on the fuhrer's anemic carcass. Dancing lightly to the edge of the stage, Hitler squatted, his back to the audience. A single sharp breath went up from the congregation at what they beheld. The face of Churchill had been tattooed around Hitler's anus. Churchill's lips appeared to pout and pucker as the fuhrer flexed his sphincter in time to the Bavarian yodel music that exploded, without warning, from the establishment's jukebox. The crowd clapped in time as their beloved führer strained, his face taking on a somewhat purple hew. With a final, superlative, effort, Hitler forced speech from Churchill. The "Churchole" addressed the audience:

> *And I in darkness unrelenting*
> *reason give—his vile venting*
> *gather round and see*
> *Unbeknownst to you, the masses*
> *I transform his pungent gasses*
> *to fine soliloquy*

The ornamented anus contorted so violently then, that even the poor and unfashionable in the pub's back rows could see its tattooed eyes bulge in supreme endeavor. Churchill's horrid maw slowly opened to remarkable diameter and vomited up an exquisite marble bust of none other than Dwight David Eisenhower. The rectum retching continued. Soon the busts of Patton, Stalin, MacArthur and Roosevelt joined Ike in an unceremonious *tribute* to the Reich's numerous enemies. Hitler's head caved in and disappeared between his shoulders. A breathtaking moment ensued as his thin body shuddered. Without warning, the fuhrer's head erupted from his distended rectum. Spitting out a mouthful of mucous the impresario dictator broke into a rousing rendition of the "Hallelujah Chorus." Genitals poured their pent-up contents into expensive trousers and lovely cocktail dresses.

Chapter 10

Salinity

P oseidon's truck was exquisite—a sporty little American vehicle with after-market wheels and big tires. Poseidon was obviously fond of vanilla. To that end he had what appeared to be no less than a dozen scented ornaments hanging from his parking-brake release handle.

Something wasn't right. As consciousness crept, like smoke through an operating suite, back into Emily's aching head, the sense of the surreal left her, replaced by a mild concern that seemed to creep unerringly toward panic. The young man at the wheel was certainly handsome and most definitely well muscled, but incontrovertibly *not* a god. She fought back a wave of gastric rebellion and, in the process, let fly a groan so soft as to be nearly imperceptible. Travis's head snapped in her direction with such force she feared it would continue all the way around and he would begin croaking out, "Fuck me! Lick me!" in a William Peter Blatty's *Exorcist* kind of way.

No such thing happened, however. Instead, with an intriguing amalgam of sheepishness and arrogance, he inquired, "Are you all right. I mean, you're not hurt, are you?"

The sincerity in his voice and mannerisms was so convincing that her fear subsided and, with piqued curiosity, Emily began, "No, I'm not hurt. Thank you. *You're* not going to hurt me, are you?" She massaged her temples and rummaged through her handbag, which Travis had gallantly placed on the floorboard before her.

"No! Certainly not! I have no intention of hurting you in any way!" His words rang impotent and stupid in his own ears. He needed to do something, to undertake some act of penance that would prove to this vision—this beautiful girl whom he desired but somehow *knew* he had no hope of ever having—that he was sincere in his remorse. He thumbed the cigarette lighter. What was the frequency of the Christian radio station in Seattle? AM five-something or other. He selected "seek" on his impressive-looking digital car stereo and froze the function as the booming voice of an evangelical Texan exploded from the dash. "Oh good woman," Travis bellowed in hot contention with the radio. "Who are all good and deserving of all my love."

"What!?" Emily's renewed concern was largely masked by the sunglasses she had produced from the beach bag, but her slackened jaw betrayed her.

"I firmly resolve with the help of thy grace to confess my sins, to do penance and to amend my life. AMEN!!!" Travis snatched the cigarette lighter from the console and stuck his tongue into it. The two of them, Travis and Emily, shrieked in titillating harmony, he in pain and she (an octave higher) in horror as the smell of burning flesh mingled with vanilla and conjured thoughts of a pork roast slathered in whipped cream. The truck swerved crazily, left the roadway and tore through a group of juvenile delinquents picking rubbish from the median. The corrections officer to whom the group had been assigned would later lose his job when an anonymous tip reported him chuckling when two maimed corpses fell from the sky, through the windshield of his Department of Corrections van, and came to rest in a post-mortem homosexual embrace in the front seat. In all, seven aspiring criminals perished. The discharged officer eventually found work in the Chicago area (as a clown at children's parties) to be lucrative beyond his dreams—the merriment of that Seattle morning never quite leaving him.

TRYPTOPHAN

Chapter 11

High (way) in the Sky (way) Free (way)

—UFO, from the 1977
Lights Out album

Matt's penis rolled out of his Bernuda shorts. Shorts had been a bad idea. Past his foot and onto the brake pedal it rolled, its weight applying sufficient pressure to seize the Isuzu Trooper's tires and send it into a high-speed skid. In desperation he twisted his body and succeeded in shifting his penis from the brake to the accelerator. Words like "crankshaft" and the proper noun "Dick Trickle" blossomed in his mind, and despite his own shock and fevered attempts to the contrary, he began to laugh out loud. A body fell from the sky, landing squarely on the Trooper's hood. Its orange reflective vest slapped out a spirited cadence against the vehicle's metallic skin. Matt's penis, which was beginning to display the first subtle signs of independent thought, rolled lazily to its left and reapplied the brakes. Outside, the corpse lurched forward and disappeared under the bumper.

A stylish white pick-up truck tore by in the opposite direction. "Send your prayer requests along with $50 to pastor Casey (*static*), care of K (*static*) radio," or something to that effect, pouring from its open windows. The vehicle's occupants seemed engaged in an inappropriate game of "hot potato." In a remarkable display of superior motoring skill, the driver of the pick-up activated the right turn signal before snapping the vehicle perpendicular to its line of travel and launching it some dozen feet, end over end, off of an overpass, and into morning rush-hour traffic.

Matt drove away, his penis plastered against the Trooper's rear window, wishing it had arms with which to applaud or a mouth with which to cheer, indeed any means of expression would have suited it.

Chapter 12

Woody Russell

Wilson woke with a deep regret for having done so. Memories popped and sputtered in his aching head like the burnt and stinking electronics of his once-proud recording suite. "Yesterday was a good day. It's after midnight and I've got you on my mind" …No, that wasn't right. That was Journey, off of the *Evolution*…or was it the *Infinity* album? Concentrating, he attempted to compose his thoughts. He raised his head from the floor. Arcs of blue static electricity leapt between his hair and the carpet. His body was numb—a six-foot funny bone with hair. With a concerted effort Wilson sat up, but this still wasn't right.

The microphone stand before which he had been lustily singing, seemingly moments before, would need replacing. A handsome ram had fallen, apparently from the void of space, through his ceiling and impaled itself on the implement. Furthermore, the beast had had the poor taste to soil Wilson's carpet in its death throws. Unfortunate. Secure in the knowledge that he himself was not seriously injured, Wilson initiated what would doubtlessly prove the most demanding clean-up of his "not as young as it used to be" life.

What he had first presumed to be ringing in his ears, some strange post-traumatic tinitis, turned out to be the microphone channel softly humming to itself. It seemed the damage to his equipment was only superficially catastrophic. Crossing the room, Wilson picked his way carefully past the tangle of damaged technical wares, giving the ram a wide berth. "Livestock...deadstock...Woodstock," he sang. For the second time in as many moments, Wilson fought back an inappropriate smile. "Could almost cut myself with wit," he muttered aloud. Chuckling, he gave the ram a push and nearly strangled with laughter as it spun down the mic stand like an oversized nut on a bolt. Having reached the mixing board, Wilson bumped up the volume on the hissing channel. The sound cleared and coagulated, "Lamb of God, you take away the sins of the world. Happy are we who are called to your supper." Wilson's eyes followed the cord from its input on the mixing board, down the table and across the floor. His laughter ceased abruptly when he saw that the cord disappeared into the hideous puncture wound in the ram's underside. The microphone lodged deep in its gut, the dead beast was waxing post-mortem theological...in English even.

Chapter 13

The Gospels of Ed and John

The power of Christ compels you! The power of Christ compels you!" It didn't seem like a very sensible plan, but Ed and Jonny had exhausted all the checklist options. Performing an exorcism on the autopilot was perhaps a bit unorthodox, but, without further complication, the failed contraption disengaged and relinquished control of the aircraft. Ed gently applied back pressure and nursed the nose of the crippled aircraft back up through the horizon and into a gentle climb. A great chorus of bleating spilled from the cargo hold. Stupid as they seemed, the sheep were surprisingly empathic.

"Want me to…?" Jonny said, inclining his head toward the baseball bat.

"Not necessary," Ed answered. "They have the right to express their relief."

As the aircraft leveled, another wave of sheep excrement lapped up between the seats and broke against the circuit breaker-laden pedestal.

"On second thought Jonny," Ed reconsidered. "Go to town." Jonny squealed with glee as he bounded down the aisle.

Thoughts of Ed's days as a rock musician poked his mind's eye. Not so much the raucous rehearsals and smoky recording sessions, but the mind-frame; the all encompassing, soul-penetrating, self-redefining attitude that elevates the true artist above the huddled, stupid masses…the unthinking livestock of humanity…the…the *sheep* of the world. An irrepressible rage began to well up in him, and Ed advanced the power levers, trimming the airplane ever so slightly nose high. The climb which ensued was barely perceptible yet still the sheep screamed. Empathy? Or was Jonny upping his batting average? Slowly, ceremoniously, Ed removed the "stand by" bat from behind his seat and made his way back to the cargo hold.

Chapter 14

Homosexual Pyro-Necro-Beastiality

W ilson opened his front door and punched his stop watch…92 minutes. Not bad. The police, Officers Luis and Pasteur, acknowledge his greeting in the gruff, business-like manner indigenous to their species and entered. Officer Luis made his way to

Wilson's kitchen and began rummaging. He found a pot and set water to boil. Officer Pasteur, in the meantime, followed Wilson into the ruined recording suite. Approaching the shaggy cadaver he began taking notes. Suddenly, as if addressing an afterthought, Pasteur unholstered his service revolver and emptied four rounds into the carcass. The sound of water spilling and mindless howling burst from the kitchen. Surprised by the gunplay, Luis had apparently spilled his experiment.

Pasteur turned to Wilson. "Protocol sir. I'll need a few moments alone with the victim."

Wilson, too horrified to protest, left the room and went into the kitchen, where he found Luis inserting a thermometer into a casserole, which had inhabited the refrigerator for more than a few days.

Pasteur frowned and begun writing out a citation. "Thou shalt not covet thy neighbor's wife. Thou shalt not commit adultery." Scripture of unknown origin wafted down the hall.

Wilson left Luis fingering a pack of bologna and returned to the recording suite to find Officer Pasteur mounted up on and copulating with the corpse. "My God, My God, why have you forsaken me? The Lord is my shepherd," exploded from the P.A.speakers as Pasteur redoubled the ferocity of his gyrations.

Crazed with panic, Wilson tore the cable from the mixing board, disabling the microphone. The resulting silence was overwhelming, and would have been complete had it not been for Pasteur's gasping recitation of the "Sermon on the Mount."

Luis appeared in silhouette against the kitchen archway, his uniform on fire. Twitching insect-like, the officer's mouth opened, allowing his sizzling tongue to roll out before he fell and rolled crazily across the floor, past Wilson and into officer Pasteur and his woolly lover. The ram's luxurious coat exploded in flames.

Pasteur was incensed. He orgasmed loudly and burned

to death. Wilson's loudspeakers crackled to life. "Thou shalt not kill! Thou shalt not kill!" The animal's eyes snapped open and it struggled mightily, managing to dislodge both the microphone stand and officer Pasteur from itself. Free though the animal was from the microphone, the commandment continued booming from the speakers. "Thou shalt not kill! Thou shalt not kill!" Turning its mighty, curled horns on the smoking corpses of the two officers, the ram gored them beyond recognition. Then, wheeling about, it fixed its eyes upon Wilson. A moment of deep, empathic understanding passed between them. Over the sudden screeching of smoke detectors, Wilson perceived a final issuance from the loudspeakers. "Lazarus, I am Lazarus."

Chapter 15

Remembering

Matt missed Fred. His face contorted painfully as the tattooist's needle tore yet again into his truly tremendous penis. At the core of the magnificent mural taking shape on his shaft was a solemn, solitary gravestone on which was carved the following epitaph:

Fred is dead
or so it seems
I killed her on the trampoline
to whom shall I address...

...My most sincere apology
for shoddy gynecology
and offer compensation
for her uterine distress?

Chapter 16

Act One

The past was, after all, the past. The house lights dimmed and a hush fell over the audience. An electric lance of cold spotlight tore through the dark and exploded around Wilson's feet. He stood alone on his luminous, elliptical island peering out at the formally attired, faceless morons, each of whom had parted with a frightful sum of money for the privilege of misinterpreting his music. He imagined the review that would appear in the "Arts and Entertainment" section of tomorrow's paper; the trash media symposium in which an over-privileged and conceivably bitter thirty-something music critic would use adjectives like "cryptic," "erudite," and "surreal" to describe the miracle of his music.

The practice of shackling so pure an ideal as music with language was an abomination beyond Wilson's reckoning. The closing of the lids, a sharp drawing of breath, or one sublime tear tracing its course over a woman's cheek—these were means of expression more suited to the delicate practice of giving shape and substance to the ideal; for bringing the intangible, if for only a fleeting moment, within the greedy, clutching grasp of humanity.

"All right you morons…you seething pool of self-replicating DNA," Wilson silently fumed. "Twist on this."

Wilson wheeled and faced his orchestra, head thrown back, arms upraised, the very portrait of detached defiance. A thin trill rose, as if from a great distance. It wavered deceptively and then grew in strength until it was lifted on a cresting wave of strings and woodwinds which bore it, ever upward, into the very rafters of the great opera house before releasing it to swoop down upon the throng.

Somewhere in the crowd a bespectacled, shaggy-headed man clenched his sphincter and scrawled the words "mesmerizingly obtuse" into a crisp notepad with a silver pen on which were engraved the words "simply mad." He then went back to contemplating the titillating concept of there perhaps being an *odd* number of breasts in the evening's audience. The gracefully darting trill turned the musical equivalent of a pirouette and exploded in a violent disgorging of brass and percussion. Huge women, morbidly obese yet beautiful of voice, rode shaking, struggling Shetland ponies onto the stage. One poor animal faltered, its femur failing under the strain, and fell, whinnying mournfully, onto its side. The pony's rider, in her desperation to rouse the beast, beat the pitiable creature with her fat fists. Alas, to no avail. Enraged, she leapt into the air (a tremendous spectacle in itself) and crashed down onto the lamentable animal. Its eyes bulged from their sockets and the pony's delicate pink tongue poked from its mouth. A jet of manure shot low across the stage and struck the pianist in his expensive, patent leather loafers. The animal gave up its life, amidst much rupture and contortion, largely unnoticed by the audience, whose attention had been diverted to center stage, where the corpulent chorus had segregated themselves into opposing factions. A hideous aria of meticulously composed scales climaxed as the two sides clashed in mock swordplay—a table laden with decadent pastries the point of their contention. A particularly unsavory diva clutched a breast, the size of which brought to mind the specter of property taxes, then suffered theatric death in a manner so convincing that many in the audience were moved to impromptu fits of applause. When the curtain came down on the opening scene of the first act, her failure to stand up and return to her dressing room brought with it the horrific realization that the diva had achieved new heights of professionalism and fallen clinically dead. The coroner's report cited pulmonary embolism as the cause of death. Wilson agonized behind the drawn curtain. He would need to improvise the remaining chorus numbers. It also came to his attention that a replacement pony would need to be found. He dispatched a page boy to secure a new animal and took immediately to feverishly altering the score.

Twenty minutes later, the curtain rose to reveal three baritone brutes stuffing an androgynous tenor into the business end of a very authentic-looking catapult. The libretto was sung in the classic Italian, but, in keeping with the custom of the western world, a translation ran in electronic subtitles above center stage. The first act's opening scene translated thusly...

chorus of brutes: "So svelte and lithe is he! See how we bear him effortlessly above our company!"

first brute: "How soft and fragrant is his skin!"

second brute: "How flaxen his hair! The sheen! I am incensed with the sheen!"

third brute: "How sickly and gaunt is this wretch! This faded evening shadow of a man. He fouls the dignity of our robust trio with his girlish flitting. The degree to which his prancing gait sickens me I cannot begin to tell. Let us slay him and be done with it! My belly is empty, and my heart longs for home. Be sensible now. Bind him well and stand clear that I may smite him against the jagged rocks yonder." (Motions toward audience)

first and second brutes: "Be not hasty brother. Let us first pet and comfort him. See how he cowers before your rage. Mercy, not wrath, will save the day. Pray, hold fast the hand which would, in anger, dash such a fair one as this against yon craggy edifice."

third brute: "Stand aside, my randy brethren. Stand clear and stand fast. Cower not as does the cur. (Motions toward the tethered tenor) And, if cower you must, cower before the prospect of cold steel." (Lays hand on hilt of sword)

The first and second brute, their unabashed regret

notwithstanding, shrink away in horror. They fawn and blow kisses toward the doomed tenor, who has swooned in his inability to face his imminent demise. The third, the steadfast brute, hews the binding rope and leaps clear as the catapult uncoils, sending the newly roused and shrieking pansy arcing gracefully through the air. The faint image of his frail form fades into the remote shadows of the great structure's upper-most reaches and disappears—a crooning specter, yet another "phantom of the opera." Brutes one and two wail out their anguish in hardy harmony. They reset the catapult and struggle to wedge themselves into the sling. Their solemn requiem rises and teeters precariously on a particularly high note. Brute number one reaches out from his confinement and slashes the new line. The mechanism's timbers creak their protest at the imposition of the danger-ously heavy load and then decide against operation. Then, without warning, the catapult's great woody arm explodes, sending a shower of splinters toward, indeed, through the sling and into the husky hides of the would-be parabolically arcing brutes. The sling sags from the crippled arm and falls catastrophically to the stage. No movement can be per-ceived therein. A puddle of evil-looking liquid begins to spread from the sling's devastated base. The stain spreads toward the splayed boots of the third brute, who stands, hands on hips, with the front of his mail corselette open. A bevy of white doves flies out from between his legs. He sings, "My cock is a roost and my ass a rookery!" The flock darts and swerves over the upturned faces of the audience and disappears into the darkness. The sound of muffled, conspicuously restrained protest wafts down from on high. Several of the doves coo in horror and swoop down out of the darkness only to collide, hissing and bubbling, with white-hot spot lights. A voice, a strangely familiar tenor, issues down from the darkness and complains vigorously about animal rights. It digresses and is soon engaged in a spirited renunciation of long rehearsals and low pay. It begins demanding union representation in lieu of the oppression it feels it has lived under for so many lean years. It continues for long moments, leading itself ever farther down the road to dismay and resignation. Sobbing emits from the rafters, and a moment later the insubstantial silhouette of the prodigal tenor appears cartwheeling through the air. He has fashioned his costume into a crude harness and hangs suspended from a length of electrical cord some twenty feet above the enthralled onlookers. He hooks his feet behind his head and swings pendulously to and fro. He begins to shit and piss and sing intricate scales as the crowd roars its approval. Wilson's arms, indeed his entire form swings and undulates in a ballet of ecstasy as the curtain falls on the first act of his sublime opera.

Outside, the marquis flashed out "Gomorra... Gomorra... Gomorra," in tireless, electric testimonial.

Chapter 17

The Edge of Obsolescence

Two miserable sheep remained standing. Jonny reared back and, with one deft swing of his bat, culled the livestock population by 50 percent. The aircraft's cavernous cargo hold fell strangely silent. The remaining animal, a delicately beautiful ewe, miraculously unfouled by the veritable ocean of blood and excrement with which the whole of the floor was covered, stood watching Jonny and Ed watch one another. The animal's baleful gaze upon them completed a circuit of terrible uncertainty. Jonny's hands relaxed, relinquishing their hold on the bat. It fell to his side, dangling precariously on the edge of obsolescence. Following suit, Ed relegated his bat to the mundane office of "cane" and used it to steady his way across the inhospitable woolen landscape separating him from the lamentable ewe. The animal's eyes turned upward as if to assess his intentions. Its gaze was soft, without reprehension, doubtlessly feminine. Ed was held, perhaps, a moment too long, in that gaze, for when Jonny spoke, seconds? minutes? later, his voice had about it the quality of a window caught in a night breeze, slamming against its frame, horrifying Ed to wakefulness. "How do the police cuff an amputee?" the crass first officer asked. The empathic tremor of the ewe's fear rocked Ed to his very foundations.

Chapter 18

KRNO

Reno was an amazing town—an exploding "Jiffy Pop" of steel and glass rising up from the burning desert. Jonny had been told that the airport was nestled in the heart of the city and could, therefore, prove elusive to the uninitiated. Flying was easy. Finding airports that were supposedly sprawling right in front of the windscreen could sometimes be difficult. Such was not the case that day. The conspicuousness of the Reno airport was analogous to the hypothetical erection of a minaret in Salt Lake City—difficult to overlook.

The freon-tainted breath of monolithic air conditioners bellowed from the snapping jaws of an automated, glass doorway. Jonny passed willingly into the mechanical maw, happy to leave his burden of heat and glare behind. Inside, the collective metabolism of life heightened to a dizzying state, oscillating between panic and ecstasy. Old women arranged themselves in long lines and strained in unison at the handles of one-armed bandits, a geriatric complement of galley slaves shackled and grunting at the oars of a great ship of greed that they propelled unfalteringly forward, cleaving the waves, the bloatings, of the sea of avarice. Their lives expired, nickel by nickel, dollar by dollar. Behind them, reinforcements stood, ever ready to take the places of those who fell, broke and disillusioned, from their stations.

An exquisitely beautiful woman leered out at Jonny from a back lit, staggeringly effective advertisement. Her delicate shoulders and perfectly airbrushed countenance rose demurely above the base of the rectangular sign she occupied. The effect drew the eye downward to ponder the alluring implication of her nudity. Blue eyes rode high over her sculpted cheekbones. Red lips, ridiculously so, and of a fullness bordering deformity, hung, suggestively parted in an eternally frozen oration of, "You, yes you, pilot boy... Fuck me." The text suspended above the carnal advertisement explained that, to do so, one needed venture to an establishment known as the "Gentlemen's Club." The euphemistically brilliant language cited the "Club" as the "ultimate venue for business or pleasure." What manner of business was undertaken there remained ambiguous.

Jonny had never completely comprehended the commodities market. What, for example, were "pork bellies?" Perhaps a junket. An educational safari to the Gentlemen's Club could redeem him from the damnation of ignorance. There could certainly be no denying an implied parallelism between such a place as the Gentlemen's Club and the suggestive implications of "pork belly." Perhaps Jonny had entirely misconstrued the concept of the pork belly. Was it indeed a verb and *not* the noun he had always supposed it to be? The fit of academia passed, and Jonny was left to marvel at the stupefying realism of the girl in the photograph. Could she be a hologram? No doubt, if questioned as to the nature of a hologram, the woman in the photo would conclude that it was an atrocity that befell the Jews of the '40s.

Chapter 19

Vivian s Oblivion

Father Vivian smiled grimly at the barista's acknowledgment that his latte was ready. He held out a painfully skeletal hand, the blue veins of which rose and fell from sight like eels in a bowl of cream, and bestowed upon the emphatically unimpressed woman a blessing that, by his reckoning, sufficed as a gratuity. She bowed her head in curt acknowledgment of the archaic gesture and gave herself over to entertaining thoughts of the good father scalding his throat and dying on the sidewalk. "Thank you, father." She conceded the pleasantry despite herself. Strict adherence to professional protocol was sometimes difficult. The frugal father, blissfully unaware of the barista's venomous, unspoken thoughts, made his way eastward, back toward the sanctuary of the St. James rectory. Could there perchance have been a common linguistic root which "rectory" and "rectum" had shared before differentiating? The shallow shriver contemplated as he sipped his coffee.

And shrive he did! Oh yes, countless multiplicities of confessions had Vivian presided over. No stranger was he to the bland sacramental monologues of suburban housewives who had in their daytime television-induced hysteria, copulated with feather dusters and screamed out the name "Fabio" only to fall whimpering into the seizures of ecclesiastical remorse. Yet these women, whose homes remained dusty despite the padre's reproach, fell shamefully short in degrees of sinfulness to the arch villains of the arch diocese—the homosexuals of Capitol Hill. The reverend father gasped now and again in horror at the confessed undertakings of some of his more "liberal" parishioners: the insertion of foam rubber footballs into rectums, the tattooing of penises and the piercing of scrotums with looping gold rings (hung for purpose of serving as "knockers" on the anus—a sort of "formal" way to request and gain access to the musty confines there of, perhaps even win a football).

The depth and breadth of their sins were an inexhaustible source of vulgar fascination for the curious clergyman. The dawning of each new day filled him with an irrepressible optimism that into his confessional would waltz that "certain special sinner" who, inspired by forces beyond understanding, had ascended sodomy's summit and found there some act, some inexplicable antic the likes of which none, not even Vivian himself had seen or heard before.

"Beg your pardon, Father!" The bicycle messenger swerved erratically and by some miracle of relative good fortune managed to steer clear of the contemplative clergyman, only to entrench his front wheel firmly in the deep, street side gutter, which led down, as all gutters do, to a yawning storm drain that seized fast his spindly machine and sent the cyclist vaulting, limp and horrified, through the plate-glass window of a prominent downtown eatery. Father Vivian, forgetting himself in the moment's upheaval, scalded his throat, much to the amusement of the spiteful barista whose musical laughter was drowned in a tumult of whooping sirens and screeching brakes as the first of the aid units arrived to administer antacids to the disgruntled diners whose early lunch had been so rudely interrupted.

Father Vivian's oblivion, inconvenient as it had been to those around him, was well founded. That morning's parade of the penitent had brought with it the cataclysmic confession for which he had so fervently longed.

Chapter 20

Grotesque Anatomy

Father Stanley had been born in Poland. A stout, strong featured Pole was he. His nose rose up from his face in a jutting leap of olfactory prominence the likes of which Jimmy Durante himself would have enthusiastically endorsed as an ideal after which genetic engineers and plastic surgeons should strive. The antithesis of the good father's superlative nose was his diminutive pouting mouth. The orifice was ghastly. A puckering, salivating puncture wound from whose depths oozed the monotonic baritone that had sedated—indeed, anesthetized—by means of voluminous sermons, countless faithful Catholics across Europe and America. The overall effect of his hideous countenance was an impression of the male organs of generation. His eyes, a pair of withered testicles, had hanging between them a magnificent, bulbous penis, which pointed ever downward toward a pungent, spastic anus, the incessant flatulence of which was ecclesiastical rhetoric.

Father Stanley had been educated in France. It was in Paris—among the world's beautiful, all drinking espresso, pissing in the streets and kissing each other in casual greeting—that he acquired the taste for boys…young boys…tender boys. The obsession began benignly enough—spying on altar boys as they changed from their street clothes into the solemn ceremonial vestments of the Catholic church. He soon began to insist that the boys bathe prior to serving mass—to cleanse from their nubile bodies the filth of a sinful world before entering God's holy of holies. The good father would, of course, observe and in many cases assist in the absolutions in his fervor to maintain the sanctity of his

Lord's sacred sanctuary. Soon he was forgetfully running his outstretched index finger over the parted lips of young men as he administered communion. One Palm Sunday, he insisted on having a particularly well-muscled young deacon beat his naked buttocks vigorously with a supple, freshly cut palm frond. The strapping youth flailed Stanley's corpulent flanks until, finally, at the conclusion of a falsetto rendering of "Ave Maria," the flogged father swooned and fell to the sacristy floor where he lay for many minutes amongst his soiled robes and indulged himself in the wild improvisation of Gregorian chants.

Back issues of *Honcho* and *Mano-a-Mano* magazines were occasionally happened upon, stripped of their covers and painstakingly recovered in *Life* and *Newsweek* livery. Conspicuously large sums of money were found to be missing from the Sunday collection baskets as Father Stanley began finding it increasingly difficult to justify the parish's acquisition of latex undergarments and equine tack. The October hay-ride was canceled when, instead of a horse, the children arrived to find Father Stanley harnessed, naked, to the hay wagon. He perspired and trembled in anticipation of tasting the driver's expertly placed whip, an evil-looking implement that he had personally chosen and listed as a "holy water baton" on the September expense report. Stanley's decline began in earnest when he took to hemming his vestments just below the knees and adopted the practice of wearing black patent leather high heels during the Saturday service and a more conservative tan flat on Sundays.

Congregational attrition finally prompted an audience with the bishop, who reportedly reprimanded Stanley for wearing earth-tone shoes with purple vestments during Pentecost. The two spent the remainder of the afternoon modeling, one for the other, the bishop's extensive spring wardrobe before adjourning to the chapel for an evening of spirited ballroom dancing. His Holiness the Bishop was pleased, in subsequent weeks, to learn that Father Stanley

DOC SOLOMMEN

had acquired an impressive cache of designer footwear, all of which coordinated with the season's pastel stoles. The tide of congregational attrition did, however, continue to crest, and Father Stanley was transferred to St. James where he would assist the pastor, Father Vivian, in his ministry to a decidedly more "liberal" parish.

Chapter 21

Act Two

Jesus Christ strode past Wilson and assumed his place at center stage. His open-front bell-bottom jump suit, elaborately embroidered with all manner of colorful rhinestones, captured the white-hot spotlight and cast it back over the audience in a prysmic explosion that left the society critics scrambling for their thesauri. He ascended a dais and held his arms aloft in triumph as he turned through 360 degrees of shameless exhibition. Leather fringe swayed gracefully beneath the costume's outstretched sleeves. Seven-inch platform heels elevated him to truly imposing stature. The platform rotated, turning him to face Wilson. Christ smiled benevolently and laid his hands on Wilson's head in loving benediction. The blessing had about it an overwhelming air of serenity. Years of hardship melted from Wilson's face. The composer's eyes suddenly ignited, radiating a vitality he'd thought long relegated to the archive of his youth. Even when Christ's hands released him, Wilson remained transfixed, his consciousness drawn introspectively about him. The crowd roared its approval as Christ completed his revolution and regarded them warmly.

From the shadows of stages left and right, apostles appeared, six to a side, adorned in the raiment of war. Close scrutiny would have revealed their mail corselets to, indeed, be made wholly of compact disc re-releases of Herb Alpert's *Rise* album.

Terrified aboriginal pygmies, captured on faraway dark continents and held in windowless crates until that very moment, were released on stage. They ran about shrieking in unadulterated horror. Two collided at a dead run and fell, unmoving, into the orchestra pit. The hybrid tribe assembled itself into a sloppy school and coursed to and fro in spastic synchronicity, the timing of their movements relative to the music, leaving much to be desired. Wilson, having regained his composure, redoubled the vigor with which he conducted his musicians. French horns bellowed in revolutionary new modes. The first chair violinist fell dead as an aboriginal spear clattered off of a trombone and pierced his throat. A pygmy, overwhelmed to the brink of pure instinct, leapt headfirst into a sousaphone. An explosion of excrement emitted from him as his life expired in a booming whole note, punctuating a particularly violent crescendo. An unusually cunning aborigine crept, splayed on all fours, nose to the floor, following the thinly masked scent of horse manure into the wings, where he found salvation in the looping, vine-like ropes that rose up into the parapets where only light and prop technicians dared go. He tested one such line for strength. Satisfied, he yelped and disappeared in a fantastic flourish of flashing extremities.

The armored apostles, meanwhile, had busied themselves with the distasteful chore of converting and sanctifying the pagan pygmies. Relentless, they pressed forward in their task. Trembling, panic-stricken tribesmen were lashed together with long strings of rosary beads and made to grunt out their new Christian names. Others were painstakingly instructed in the cryptic "sign of the cross" ritual in which one recites, "In the name of the Father and of the Son and of the Holy Spirit," while touching his right hand to first the forehead, then the heart and left and right sides of the breast respectfully. Many of the reluctant converts took readily to

the exercise while still more were left blinded, dirty fingers stuck in their eyes, rolling about the floor shrieking, "Michael, Thomas, Philip." Others, not especially expedient on the uptake, inserted thumbs into their rectums and hopped about, eyes rolled back in mad confusion howling out "Fatherson-o-lysprit" in vulgar displays of sacrilege.

A statue of Saint Joseph was wheeled onto the stage. A child in one of the exclusive, hideously expensive front-row seats leapt up pointing and shouting, "G.I. Joe! G.I. Joe!" His mother gently suppressed his enthusiasm, pointing out to him that the stone effigy was, in reality, that of Jerry Garcia. She closed her eyes and began to hum "Casey Jones" softly to herself. The child returned to brooding while, two rows back, a near-sighted crone dismissed the plausibility of what, to her, seemed a fleeting glimpse of an aboriginal tribesman abducting an expensively attired child and ascending a rope into the opera house's darkened heights.

Two lesbians in elaborate costume garb, one a baker, the other a North Sea fisherman, wheeled carts onto the stage and began to toss loaves of bread and whole whitefish at Christ, who deftly caught and juggled seven of each. The crowd erupted in a fit of applause so raucous as to drown even the fanfare of trumpets that accompanied Jesus's juggling. Christ blushed and speaking in subdued tones into the nearest microphone declared, "Thou hast seen yet nothing." He flung the fish-bread medley out over the crowd where it disappeared, imploding with no more than a delicate *POP* to mark its passing.

Six people in the throng, all of them allergic to sea-food, fell dead to the sticky floor. The remainder of the assembly were left rubbing their full stomachs in engorged contentment. Gluttonous belches accompanied uproarious applause.

Chapter 22

Off Time On the Off Ramp

T
ravis woke with a start and was immediately aware of the unfathomable power he possessed. That awareness and an unrelenting sense of brooding bitterness spurred and mercilessly goaded the cancerous remnant of his former self to expire, thus delivering him over to the wholeness of the ancient evil of which he was now incarnate.

Emily, instinctively aware of some cataclysmic upheaval in the very fabric of reality, struggled to open her remaining eye. She saw before her, in the final moment of her short life, the new Travis. He was unharmed. In point of fact, he was resplendent. Feeling her eyes upon him, Travis turned to face the critically wounded girl. Sensing her vulnerability, he pursed his lips at her and gently inhaled. Emily felt her life being torn, like a weed by its roots, from her body and out into nothingness. Rolling her essence about on his tongue, Travis savored the lass's wholesomeness before savagely biting down on and swallowing up that which, in another existence, he might have loved.

An arriving state patrol officer, long jaded by his sobering profession, found only one corpse in the wreckage and, seeing the impression of final and absolute terror on her face, wept openly.

Chapter 23

The Misfortunes of Todd

Todd, had he been of sufficient intellect to do so, would have recognized himself for the uneducated, vulgar white trash he was and, seeing the unattractive truth, undertaken the only logical course of action available to him—throwing himself into an industrial meat grinder at the packing plant where he toiled, semi-diligently, in an ongoing effort to sustain the opulent beer-swilling, dart-throwing lifestyle to which he was accustomed. Sadly, Todd had only rudimentary intelligence and absolutely no self-identity. He, therefore, went on living.

With the plodding focus of a crocodile rolling down an embankment into a muddy river to feed, Todd steered his shabby yellow Toyota pickup out of his weed-strangled front lawn, through a culvert and out of sight—off on yet another junket to the slaughter house. His wife (a distant cousin) and their brood of disease-carrying offspring stood waving on the porch, watching the "Jimmy Buffet for President" bumper sticker-encrusted jalopy disappear into rush-hour traffic. Mother looked forward to her customary day of talk shows punctuated by infomercials all washed down with ice-cold beer, while the children, for their own parts, eagerly anticipated 24 more hours of malnutrition and neglect punctuated by an offhand beating or two in preparation for the main event—the evening beatings at Dad's hands and the fresh-from-the-microwave box of pizza pockets they would enjoy before being shipped off to bed to lie cowering in mute horror at the prospect of a special "midnight visit" from Dad and his ironically labeled "family sized" can of vegetable shortening.

Chapter 24

Pardon Me, But...

Travis entered the new car show-room singing Queen's "I'm in Love with my Car." Freddie Mercury wheeled in his sarcophagus as Travis expanded his effort into a medley concluding with "Bohemian Rhapsody's" solemn "Mama, I just killed a man" stanza. The five salesmen on duty frothed, simultaneously, at the mouth and, after having produced and handed Travis the keys to each and every car on the lot, including their own, seated themselves quite comfortably in a shining and terribly expensive mini van. The sales manager himself assumed the driving responsibilities. Travis bowed low and presented the ignition key, which the manager accepted, guided home and smartly turned. A whisper of electronic ignition later, the practical family vehicle surged forward through the dealership's cleverly painted, plate-glass showroom window and was lost from sight in an explosive impact with the service building...a spectacle of truly Oppenheimerish proportions.

Travis, in the meantime, had selected a green convertible Mustang GT and was perusing the owner's manual with glee.

Chapter 25

Friday in the P.M.

Todd fingered the sealed envelope that contained, in the form of a crisp paycheck, an entire Friday evening's worth of relief from matrimonial and paternal obligations. The condemning looks shot brazenly at him by a pair of elderly women stopped behind him at a traffic light had no discernible effect on the delirious hillbilly. He stared ahead, blissfully oblivious, into realms with which only he and perhaps a precious few severely overworked and starving African cattle were familiar. He pondered in those moments the phenomenally mysterious physiological process by which breath escaped the lungs and left the body via the anus. He unconsciously contracted and drew in his abdomen in a half-hearted attempt to reverse the process and breathe rectally. Failing, he managed only an exhalation, the halitosis of which shocked him back to the confounding reality of two silver-haired women honking and cursing as they laboriously maneuvered their 1974 Chevy Malibu around his stationary truck. "Fuck you. And fuck Jimmy Buffet, too!" cried the shotgun granny between surprisingly deft exhibitions of a knotty, arthritic pair of middle fingers. "You redneck asshole!" she concluded as the Malibu disappeared around a corner.

"Long-neck, ice cold," Todd pondered. "Sounds good!" And he wove his way to a favorite tavern.

Chapter 26

Things To Do In a Malibu

The black leviathan rounded a corner, whitewalls squealing in protest, and came to a lurching stop along-side a gleaming convertible Mustang. The sportscar's emerald, metal flake paint, polished to a ridiculously high gloss, reflected the Malibu's rather unimaginative lines in an inspired distortion, that was a decided improvement on the 20/20 original.

The Malibu's elderly occupants giggled girlishly while allowing their eyes to casually linger on the strapping, shirtless lad at the Mustang's helm. A bronze Isuzu Trooper pulled up beside and to the left of the black Chevy and, to the overt delight of the randy grandmothers, was occupied by a grave-looking but lean and handsome boy whose time in the world could surely not have exceeded 18 years.

Bifocals were adjusted and volumes of expensive but tasteless lipstick were hastily applied in an effort to secure the young man's attention—and secure it they did. The lad in the Mustang, turning to face his admirers, tilted his sunglasses up to reveal a pair of smoldering pits from whose depths rose the vapors of despair. The women's minds were seared with images of their respective gravestones, the dates of their deaths outlined and emphasized in gaudy lipstick. Between the two freshly turned patches of earth grew a magnificent lilac bush. A dog, by closest estimation, huge in stature, shaven and tattooed, diseased…armored in sores, some of which puckered and pouted in weeping discharge of viscous infectant, emerged from the vegetation and lifted its leg. An enormous caricature of a penis unfurled with a sound not unlike that of a New Year's party horn and rained an unsavory irrigation on the lilac. The beast's yawning, toothed maw opened and the sound of children weeping belched from its gut. The lilac withered and died. On either side of the now forlorn bush, shrunken skeletal heads emerged from the rich brown soil. Lipstick-smeared teeth parted as brittle mandibles clacked out, "Wash away my iniquity and cleanse me of my sin."

In a final act of supreme effort, the women, sisters, truth be told, tore their eyes from the green demon steed. Their lolling heads rolled in unison to the left where a colossal penis was pressed against the Trooper's passenger side window in apparent desperation to roll it down and speak its mind.

Chapter 27

A Will and a Way

G uilt breeds desperation and so it was that Matt, having become a stranger to solace, found himself at the door of his long-time companion and trusted friend Will. Several minutes of laborious knocking proved fruitless, the effort drowned and wasted in the senseless whirring of an expensive Moulinex food processor. A detour to the ground-floor apartment's kitchen window and some rigorous rapping had the desired effect, however, and moments later Matt and Will sat, facing one another, in solemn council.

"I loved her because she let me have my darkness." Matt began. "So many, before her, demanded I maintain a naiveté, a childlike optimism and acceptance of humanity that, despite my heroic efforts to the contrary, was easily recognizable as a belabored facade and drove the relationship to ruin. Fred was unique, wonderful. She accepted my darkness and cynicism as evolutionary adaptations that facilitated not so much my existence, but my sanity. Strange thing sanity: the obscure, intangible standard that none can clearly define but any can recognize a lack of."

An egg timer sounded and Will, leaping from his chair, motioned for Matt to follow. He crossed the foyer and slid expertly into his kitchen. Matt carefully seated himself in one of the dining room chairs, all of which had, sadly, dwindled into frightening stages of disrepair, and watched in rapt amazement as Will extracted a conspicuously perfect soufflé from his beloved oven. "Viola!" he exclaimed as he presented his creation. Matt, though thoroughly impressed, politely declined his friend's offer of lunch and returned to his macabre reminiscing.

A sound, a horrible, frightening sound, resembling the peeling of thunder or the racket of a stampeding herd of ponies, rolled through the apartment. Will twitched in stupefied horror as his soufflé was shaken from the edge of the dining room table and fell to ruination. Matt grew dizzy and disoriented as vast volumes of blood rushed to and distended his colossus. The ceiling immediately above them bulged as if some intolerable load had been imposed upon it. In an instant of bewildering kinesis, the joists and flooring above gave way, and Will's neighbor, a leviathan of a women, poured down from the structural laceration. She crashed through and reduced the glass dining room table to shards. Were it not for the fact that Will's was a ground-floor dwelling, situated firmly on an immense and sturdy slab of solid concrete, the meaty meteorite might well have passed through yet another floor and continued on to a gruesome demise at the very molten center of the planet. Her ample buttocks bled lustily as she gathered herself up in an Herculean effort and grunted out what, to Matt, seemed a prophetic utterance. "When is it over? When is it really all over?" Her small but powerful hands darted out and groped Matt's engorged phallus which, to Matt's horror and Will's fascination, spoke.

"Back! Unhand me, greybeard loon!" it snarled. Eloquent though it was, quoting Coleridge, actually, the prick was obviously quite blind. The husky house-frau spoke no more. Her life expired in a series of nonsensical mutterings, all of which had some inference or another to fast food.

"Jesus," muttered Will. "Look at the size of her ass."

"Caverns measureless to man," quoted the well-spoken penis. At the edge of consciousness, Matt pondered the meaning of the fat woman's last words.

DOC SOLOMMEN

Chapter 28

Obscene Latrine

The back issue of *Honcho* magazine proved worth the $12.95 it had cost Father Stanley. For as long as the randy priest could recall, the Sudlack family's Sunday envelope, had, without fail, contained a crisp 20-dollar bill. A simple instance of clerical intercession and a covert trip to the letter box had laid the groundwork for the sublime masturbatory exercise which, under the guise of constipation, Stanley had just concluded for the sixth time. He absently searched the toilet side magazine rack for a newspaper or perhaps an issue of *National Geographic* in which to conceal his lewd periodical, then paused, frozen in rapt admiration of the full-page advertisement exploding from the Sunday paper's Arts and Entertainment insert.

The graphic depicted three beautifully muscled youths manhandling a smaller individual of indeterminate gender. In the background a titanic catapult presided over an assemblage of equestrians, all of who seemed distracted by some religious artifact set on a small altar. *Gomorra,* an opera by Russ Wilson, loomed—the only text on the otherwise purely symbolic show bill. Stanley's small eyes poured repeatedly over the advertisement. His pupils dilated and the smallest rivulet of drool descended from his slackened lips only to be drawn smartly back in by the sharp inhalation that signified his return to reality.

Father Vivian's insistent rapping on the bathroom door squelched any fledgling thoughts of pulling off a seventh time, and Stanley unleashed a sortie of coughs and sniffles to mask the tell-tale sound of shuffling pages as he rolled his visual aids together into an innocent looking packet, then rose to move his industry to a less frequented area of the rectory.

The following Sunday, the Sudlack family's envelope financed a night at the opera. (Additional apologies to Freddie Mercury.)

Chapter 29

Zoos and Other Groovy Places

I f asked for his opinion regarding zoological gardens, Travis would have confessed a marked preference for museums. Everything in a museum was blissfully dead—and therefore wonderfully cooperative in matters of conspicuousness. For example, there was no having to wander outdoors in vain pursuit of an indecisive tapir. The museum tapir had not only been dead since 1956, but was stuffed, fitted out with glass eyes and bolted to the concrete base of a very stationary display case—a study in spectator convenience. Sadly, Seattle had not a single museum of natural history. The city's naturalistically inclined had no choice but to make due with safariing through the Woodland Park Zoological Gardens. Woodland Park was, however, a respectable zoo. Travis liked the natural environs in which the specimens were displayed particularly. Having gained admittance at the expense of a 22-year-old gate attendant who suffered a medically inexplicable cerebral hemorrhage, Travis made his way to the "Savanna Overlook." This was an impressive exhibit. Ten acres of lush grassland girded with a man-made "canyon," which served nicely as a deterrent to any of the exhibit's numerous creatures which may have contemplated escape. Vast water holes and towering beobob trees punctuated a meticulous recreation of the African flat-lands. Zebras moved in meandering aimlessness, perpetually changing course to avoid undesirable conflicts with hippos, which emerged from and disappeared into a great central pool at unpredictable intervals. Giraffes loped about, continuously on the alert for the hay wagon that appeared, unlike the hippos, with unwavering regularity.

It was Tuesday. The animals were, of course, unaware of this. They did, however, fathom that this was the day during which their uncontestedly favorite keeper, Joel, would arrive not only with the noon hay, but a bushel of apples and perhaps even a sack of oatmeal. By 11:30 a.m., anticipation had reached a fever pitch. Hippos rose and sank like prowling submarines in their murky pool, their desire for oatmeal surpassing even their intolerance of the oppressive midday heat. Zebras darted and bucked in striped suspense while a troop of baboons found voice and raised a simian revile of which Noah himself would have disapproved.

Joel noted with no small satisfaction that his entrance into the compound corresponded exactly with his watch's aural annunciation of the noon hour. Lumbering up a cleverly concealed access ramp and into the enclosure, his utility vehicle struggled mightily beneath the weight of 30 bales of hay, no fewer than four bushels of apples and an institutionally-sized canister of oats. The zebras, swiftest of the exhibit's inhabitants, crowded around the lunch wagon in unmitigated glee. The throng advanced with such enthusiasm that Joel was hard-pressed to force his way from the vehicle's cab and up onto its bed where he began, among many a hearty whoop and whistle, the work of distributing the booty to his beloved charges.

Straw flew in all directions and apples were merrily thrown to myriad grateful creatures of the savanna. Neither man nor beast, in their fervor, noticed the strapping lad who watched them and their carryings on so intently from the shelter of one of the many observation huts situated about the exhibit's perimeter. Nor did they notice the subtle change in Earth and atmosphere as the beaming sun gave way, faltered and perished in the sudden and unnaturally violent gathering and advance of storm clouds touched with the ominous hues of deep and stagnant water. A long, searching finger of lightning reached down from one such cloud and tickled the heaving surface of the hippo pool. The two animals immersed therein—a riotously enormous cow and her suckling calf—found themselves dead and orphaned, respectfully. The sparse smattering of zoo-goers present for the spectacle reeled in horror as the mammoth cow ruptured and exploded two feet below the surface of the pool. The transformation of the water from pale green to electric red was instantaneous.

Around the corner, in the reptile house, irrational feelings of inadequacy plagued a contemplative chameleon.

Organs of every discipline and yards of sinew bobbed crazily between islands of hide and hair. The infantile hippo had, in the meantime, been jettisoned cleanly from the confines of the exhibit and landed some 12 blocks away in an intersection within clear view of a Metro bus stop. The commuters huddled beneath the stop's small roof moaned morosely, and anticipated a long delay in their commute as the 174 Highway 99, Sea-Tac Airport bus smashed furiously into the large gray pig J-walking across Fourth avenue.

The smell of death wafted up from the hippo pool and spread in an insidious cloud across the acres of cultivated confinement.

Distracted from its grooming regimen by the sudden sensory smorgasbord, a careless baboon inadvertently plucked the eye of its troop's dominant male from its socket, thereby sending the terminally enraged primate on an incensed killing spree that began, appropriately enough, with the offending baboon and ended in shocking suddenness when the partially blinded animal, deprived of its depth perception, misjudged the span of the encircling canyon and leapt to a dramatic, if not graceful, death on the rocks below. It expired miserably, face up, with the day's last lingering ray of sunlight offending its remaining eye.

Overhead, the maturing storm clouds began to congregate in earnest. Calamitous thunderclaps—sounds unheard since the Earth's infancy—rumbled ominously. Obscene, probing tongues of lightning danced across and ignited vast expanses of the exhibit's grasses. Horrified zebras dashed one another senseless with savage kicks and bolted in segregated bands to unique demises. One group, stampeding madly, careened over the lip of the yawning canyon and compiled a mound of such intricate lines and patterns that Escher himself would have succumbed to vertigo. A second group galloped headlong into the fouled hippo pool and was decimated in the jaws of a raging bull hippopotamus, that was failing in its attempt to cope with the loss of its mate and the disappearance of its heir.

The third, final and most dramatically accomplished group expired amidst much twitching and hissing as it vainly mounted a disorganized offensive against an expanse of electrical fencing.

Joel was beside himself with horror at the seemingly inexplicable occurrences. Fixing his eyes upon the zookeeper, Travis exerted the full force of his will on the unsuspecting chap. Joel's sanity slipped away and dissipated in thin vapors from his nostrils and eyes. Aeons of evolutionary refinement were systematically repealed until, overcome by long-forgotten drives and desires, Joel tore away his beloved uniform, sprouted a sudden and abundant growth of beard, squatted, pissed on his territory and recklessly leapt into the barrel of apples, which he lustily devoured before moving on to consume 15 pounds of oats. He died of constipation, a week later, in an insane asylum, his digestive tract unable to cope with the cataclysmic influx of dietary fiber.

Travis tired of the zoo and made his way toward the main exit. There, posted on a public reader board, he spied a fascinating show bill.

Chapter 30

Craters and Other Smoking Holes

I t had taken no fewer than six staunch state troopers to move the tattered and seeping carcass out from Will's dining room and onto a pathetically inadequate gurney, which had, at least, had the good taste to creak out its protestations before collapsing. A makeshift sling, fashioned entirely from gun belts, was devised and employed to drag the corpse, which dredged a frightfully deep furrow across Will's otherwise impeccable lawn, up and into the coroner's van. The vehicle listed and made a series of ugly noises before reluctantly accepting the load.

A cursory examination of the floor above Will's apartment failed to disclose any apparent shortcomings in design or construction. The property manager, amid much apologizing and repeated assurances of swift repairs and prorated rent, had made arrangements for Will to reside at a rather posh downtown hotel for at least the next two nights.

Having gathered a sparse assortment of bare essentials, Will took his leave of the apartment which had, for so long, been his home. Had he known he would never again set eyes upon his home, Will would, perhaps, have allowed himself the indulgence of a lingering, sentimental survey of the space. As things were, however, he did, without so much as a backward glance, climb into his truck and with Matt, still uncharacteristically silent and brooding in the seat

beside him, speed off into the orange surrealism of a thousand argon vapor streetlights.

The long, uncomfortably silent minutes finally aggravated Will into sympathy for his confused and morose friend. "When the fat lady sings." Will's voice seemed unnaturally loud and abrasive in the cab that had been as silent as a morgue. Matt's failure to give adequate response prompted Will to clarify, "It's over when the fat lady sings, you stupid fuck."

"She won't be doing much singing from here on out," came Matt's retort.

"Not necessarily her. The cliché alludes to opera."

"Yeah, yeah, yeah, I understand that much. It's still vague," Matt shot back.

Will resigned himself to indifference. "Just let it ride, man. We'll get some sleep and hopefully, some perspective, and maybe in the morning some pieces will fall into place."

They smiled together at the unintended pun and continued northward, toward the city proper, in a much more amiable silence.

Chapter 31

On Plumbing

F ather Vivian followed the progress of a moth across the vibrant backdrop of his television screen and wondered what manner of sensory overload the insect must have been experiencing. A floor above, the bathroom door closed and locked for the third time since the beginning of the mindless half-hour sitcom that even the moth had likely predicted the conclusion of. The apparent severity of Stanley's constipation set Vivian's mind into agitated, involuntary activity.

164

TRYPTOPHAN

Expenses seemed to have taken a sharp upward turn since Stanley's arrival at St. James. The water bill had nearly tripled and the profusion of miscellaneous "acquisitions" on the monthly expense reports was breeding suspicions and fostering incessant, disturbing suppositions about the reclusive new assistant pastor. Vivian had initially dismissed Stanley's odd comings and goings at positively abhorrent hours and his penchant for viscous, semi-solid foods like pudding, Jell-O and CheezeWhiz, as eccentricities resultant from a European education and the micromandibular condition from which the puckering padre's face suffered. The events of the last week were, however, bizarre beyond even Vivian's rational. Rising slowly, as if against his own will, Vivian crossed the television illuminated study and extracted from an expanse of handsome cherry wood shelving the inauspicious leather-bound volume that contained his ongoing journal. Having found the entry pertaining to the preceding Saturday, he steeled himself and read the incredulous account of events therein.

He had been awakened from an exquisite dream in which the Pontiff, choking to death on an errant bone in his whitefish fillet, was scrawling Vivian's name, in tartar sauce, onto a richly embroidered napkin in a desperate, dying effort to recommend him as his successor. Without warning, a percussive overture, unknown since mid-century Hiroshima, exploded outside his window. Surprise and shock sent Vivian vaulting from his Spartan bed at a bone jarring velocity of which his chiropractor would later write "conceivably contributed to periods of dizziness and incontinence." Vivian's bed didn't remain vacant long, however, insomuch as, no sooner had the frightened father picked himself up from his floor, than an evil, unattractively dented aluminum garbage can tore, with malicious ferocity, through the room's street side-window and came, amid much flying goose down, to a violent splash-down in the very spot the good father had, mere seconds ago, comfortably occupied.

The small room relinquished its customary cleanliness, its intensive infusion of incense and wood polish wilting under the olfactory onslaught of spoiled meat and rancid butter—the refuse of last week's parish pancake breakfast. Vivian's composure failed, and he lapsed into anguished wailing, unconsciously mimicking the sudden blaring of a car horn just outside his window. Barely perceptible beneath the din, a car door creaked open on ruined hinges. A pair of stiletto-heeled feet descended from the devastated automobile and tested, then tentatively crunched across the glass-littered driveway, stopping at the rectory door. Angry hissing evinced the disgorging of electrolytes and amid a shower of sparks and impressive plumes of acrid blue smoke, the car's battery, and mercifully its horn, surrendered their symbiotic lives.

A suggestively lewd falsetto voice piped out alternating choruses of "Holy Holy Holy Lord" and "In the Navy" as Stanley began to pound vehemently at the door. "The Lord is my locksmith! I shall not want for ingress!" He bellowed. "He leadeth me this way and leadeth me that way...Have you ever seen a savior go this way and that?" Vivian was remotely aware of the warm liquid that had begun, suddenly, to cascade down his leg.

Stanley, in the meantime, entertained thoughts of marching around the house until the door fell in. Dismissing the notion on the premise that it required excessive effort, he returned to the calamity that had been his Bonneville, and extracted a rusty tire iron from its trunk. Grimacing purposefully, he pranced in grim determination to the rectory's front door. "The Lord God commands you to open before me," he shrieked. "The martyrs and the saints command you!"

Vivian, paralyzed with horror and stupefaction, remained in his bed chamber and offered no response to Stanley's challenge...save an inaudible recitation of The Lord's Prayer.

"So be it," exclaimed Stanley after a drawn out moment. Thrusting one beautifully manicured hand down the front of his leggings and brandishing the brutal tire iron in the other, the lunatic Stanley began hewing his way through the rectory's intricately ornamented front door. "You are my rod and my staff! You are my rod and my staff!" The psalm continued in mindless repetition until, with a climactic effort Stanley simultaneously gained access to the modest structure's foyer and fouled his tights. The latter being borrowed from a young man of dubious repute—supposedly a dental hygienist (with access to any number of diabolical oral probes) with whom Father Stanley had, earlier that evening, cavorted to a shameful degree. Anal intercourse had been preceeded by painful but exciting Novocain injections and the wanton inhalation of nitrous oxide. The torrid duo's post sodomy recreational activities had included an intimate episode of heroin usage and large-scale Percodan dosing. Thusly fortified, Stanley transcended his sedentary state of being and found within himself not only the will, but a raging desire to sequester himself in a well-lighted restroom and gorge himself on the ocular entrée that was the *Gomorra* show bill.

Having surmounted the troublesome front door obstacle, Stanley bounded up the stairs and dashed into his pastel floral print ornamented boudoir. Retrieving a beloved, if not somewhat wrinkled, sheet of newsprint, he retraced his steps, back down the stairwell and past Father Vivian's door where he paused, adjusted his wig, retouched his lipstick and rouge, then bid his superior, "Good evening." He then bounded off and disappeared from sight in dramatic echoes of slamming doors and flushing toilets.

Vivian's next recountable thoughts did not occur until early the following morning when he was mercilessly torn from sleep's arms a second time by a broken squelching of police band radio transmissions that issued from the yawning void in which his front door had once hung. Visible beyond the mound of splintered wood and uprooted shrubbery, the fractured grille of Stanley's Pontiac grinned postmortem sheepishness. "Excuse me, Father. Are you all right?" Vivian shielded his eyes against the rising sun's glare and mutely motioned for the young police officer to enter what must surely have been the closing chapter of a fantastic nightmare. Circumnavigating the debris, the policeman made his way toward the bewildered priest. Vivian accepted the man's outstretched hand and, with considerable assistance, took painfully to his feet. The priest's words of thanks trailed away in ugly diphthongs, and both men's faces twisted in revulsion as Stanley emerged from the lingering shadows at the top of the stairs.

He stood in three-quarter profile, adorned in the vestment and habit of a Franciscan nun. He had, however, lent what he perceived to be an air of sophistication to the ensemble by wearing his underclothing on the outside. And what striking, luxurious underclothes they were! A satin demi-bra, peach in color and perfect in fit, rode high above matching garters and thong panties. Cream hosiery tapered gracefully to a remarkable pair of white patent leather engineer's boots. The overall effect was superlatively schizophrenic, and drew the eye away from what Stanley considered his problem areas, namely his midsection and slightly overstated ankles. He descended the stairs, the very picture of poise and elegance, head tilted back, arms slightly outstretched with palms down and index fingers pointing enigmatically heavenward. Gliding past his bewildered audience, he crossed the street to the church where, still rather woozy from the Percodan, he mistook his paisley-bound prayer book for his plaid one and inadvertently performed last rights on a group of second graders who were supposed to receive the sacrament of First Holy Communion.

The backlash of parental protest began immediately and, by the following Sunday morning, news of the clerical catastrophe had spread like leprosy through the parish. Only a small group of Alzheimer's sufferers from the local rest home were present that particular week to witness a resplendent Father Stanley and two rather nervous-looking altar boys perform an elaborate mass. Father Stanley, in retrospect, thought it one of his finest.

Chapter 32

Improvisation

Wilson woke from a dream in which he was composing his masterpiece at a small desk situated squarely in the center of the Seattle Opera House's sprawling main stage. He came abruptly to the disturbing conclusion that doing so was analogous to cooking in the dining room and abandoned the effort accordingly. Rising from the desk, he took up a cumbersome vendor's harness from the floor beside his stool and spent the remainder of the night systematically walking the labyrinth of empty aisles, tossing hot dogs against vacant seats.

Chapter 33

Madison Street Memoirs

Unsure of which end of the electronic key card to insert into the receptacle on his door and wishing earnestly for an old-fashioned metal key, Will stabbed aimlessly at the mechanism's slot until he coaxed from it a Yuletide green light and the unmistakable clunking of tumblers granting him access to the suite of rooms his property management company had, so generously, provided him. The subdued lighting and freshly turned sheets incited within him a rush of adrenaline which, for reasons beyond his capacity to comprehend, he experienced in both hotels and above average restaurants.

Matt, failing to find any cause for exuberance, fell forlorn and exhausted into the bed nearest the door. He stared blankly at the smoke detector above him, alternately blinking his left and right eyes, absently fascinated by the way the circular white plastic gadget seemed to shift position. Allowing his jaw to drop to its fully extended position and poking out his tongue, he let out a hyena-like cackle which, were it not for the double thick walls, would have brought a detachment of hotel security personnel.

Chapter 34

Repercussions

Todd seemed to recall a figure of 8.0 percent as being the standard against which sobriety was measured. He concluded that the Washington State Legislature had been reasonable in pronouncing eight percent the maximum legal blood alcohol content for drivers, and finished his ninth beer. For his own part, Todd was quite sure that he could not, at the moment, have drunk himself beyond 5 percent BAC. Confident in his physical ability and his legal right to assume control of an automobile, he left the Hanging Bullet tavern and staggered across the largely deserted parking lot toward the citrus-hued "trucklette" which was his pride and joy.

"Mother fucker!" *jingle jangle* "Mother fucker!" *jingle jangle*. Key after tarnished key was fumbled for, appraised and jabbed in the general vicinity of the vehicle's ignition

TRYPTOPHAN

switch until, finally, one such large, plastic capped "Toyota" specimen slid into place and, in one of technology's small miracles, brought the dirty little truck to sputtering life. "Yahoo," "Hee-haw," and similar expressions, which were neither nouns, verbs, adjectives nor adverbs, erupted from the cab's darkened recesses as Todd's buggy lurched into traffic and traced a dubious, serpentine path down the thoroughfare and out of sight. Twenty minutes later Todd signaled a right turn, executed one to the left and audibly breathed his relief. "Almost home." He rejoiced.

Unwelcome and without warning, fast-advancing halogen headlamps glared like condemning eyes in Todd's smudged rearview mirror. A compound profanity fouled the air as Todd eased his foot from the accelerator and groped about for his seat belt. The pursuing headlamps matched the truck's velocity and hung tauntingly, a car length behind.

"Toying with me...the sonofabitch!" Todd growled. The first beads of perspiration, cloudy and reeking of alcohol, cascading down his forehead into bloodshot eyes. Fortified by the potent elixir of fear, alcohol and anger, Todd hung his great bushy head out the window and snarled. "Shit or get off the pot, you jackass motherfucker!"

The exclamation, enunciated in an interesting dialect of Hick, rang in Travis's ears like an overdue invitation. Over the course of the last several miles Travis had repeatedly found himself precariously close to the foul yellow truck's bumper-sticker encrusted rear end as its driver, obviously intoxicated, randomly varied his speed from 70 to 15 miles per hour. The game was wearing Travis's patience dangerously thin. Passing the unpredictable Toyota was entirely  out of the question given the wide, arcing detours from his lane in which its drunken driver seemed to delight in. The cursing though, the rude, inexcusable, "Shit or get off the pot, motherfucker," episode marked the breaking point of Travis's restraint.

A savage stomp on the green sporstcar's accelerator sent

it leaping forward in a break-neck burst of liberating speed. Within seconds, Travis and Todd had exchanged perspectives in a game of automotive leap frog in which the confused and enraged Todd was sorely ill-equipped to compete. Travis felt the throbbing of rage at this temples subside as the Toyota's single staring headlight dwindled and disappeared behind him. By the time he eased the Mustang (of which he was growing increasingly fond) into the car port adjacent his opulent home and extinguished the rumbling engine, Travis had regained his composure and all but forgotten the ugly incident.

Beyond any and all rational belief, the sound of clattering valves heralded the apparition of a lone headlight at the top of Travis's long, descending driveway. An ill-kept, yellow Toyota truck followed behind, cresting the rise of Travis's property and careening down the drive. The unattractive vehicle came to a lurching stop scant inches from the Mustang's rear bumper. Travis stood in mute bewilderment. Over the whistling and whining of poorly maintained accessory belts and the "twang" of the local country radio station came Todd's eloquent greeting. "Hey asshole." Travis held his ground, transfixed by the interloping motorist's simian social awareness and ignorant brazenness. "Where the fuck do you get off driving that way in a neighborhood?"

"Beg your pardon?" Travis found his voice.

"Don't 'beg your pardon' me, you little prick," Todd fumed. "Where do you get off passing me going 70 miles-an-hour on a street where my kids play?" Travis contemplated a response but thought it better to save reason for the reasonable. He chose, instead, to turn the tide of the predicament in the direction of his own personal amusement.

"I'm very sorry sir," Travis apologized with overt sarcasm. "We...my girlfriend and I, have tickets to the opera tonight. You see, if one fails to arrive on time to an opera he will not be permitted entry. The house doors will be closed and remain so until intermission. Only then are stragglers allowed to enter the…"

"Like I give a fuck about your opera!" Todd exploded. "What are you going to do when you run over some kid, you asshole?"

Travis felt anger break painfully, then spill warm over his soul. "I guess I'd do a little time in jail, Todd."

Todd, lost and senseless with rage, failed to notice Travis's deliberate use of his given name and went on. "Yeah! Maybe that's what you need, Mr. I live in a big expensive house and drive a little convertible sportscar motherfucker. Maybe you need to go to the big house and get fucked in your ass for a few years, get knocked off your high-horse."

A final attempt at civility on Travis's part. "Sir, I assure you, I don't normally drive in that fashion. I will be more conservative in…"

"My ass! I always see that goddamn car driving around here like that," Todd went on, gesturing toward the green Mustang. "Why you son of a…" The drunk's words echoed and faded from Travis's perceptive field.

"Always sees this car driving around here like that? How could that be?" Travis wondered as he began to muster his concentration.

"If it was up to me I would…" The ongoing rant abated, then ceased altogether as Todd, short on intellect but almost sheep-like in instinct and empathy, sensed a disquieting change.

"You would what, Todd?" Travis's question was calm, detached in tone, but keen in effect. "What would you do, Todd?" he pressed. Crossing the distance between himself and the substantially larger, older and suddenly unsure (frightened) man in three brisk strides, Travis seized the trespasser in an icy, inhuman glare. Suddenly realizing Travis's usage of his name, Todd endeavored a weak and tentative retort.

"Why I'm going to..." Todd staggered against his truck in shock and disbelief as Travis finished his sentence.

"...to beat your smart little ass and teach you a lesson, son!" Travis's lips moved, but it was Todd's own voice that issued from between them. "And after I'm done with you, I'm going to knock back that last longneck I've got stashed under my seat, drive home and finish the cold chicken in the fridge, tell my kids and old lady how I kicked a rich little asshole around and then, when the kids are back in bed, I'm gonna have the wife blow me in front of the TV while I watch *Three's Company* reruns. Can't wait!" Travis resumed in his own voice. "Is that about the gist of it, Todd? Does that about sum up the crackle of short circuits you mistakenly call *thoughts* tear assing around your sorry head?"

Tears and snot poured from Todd's eyes and nostrils as the hair was burned from his nose in a tragedy that would condemn him to a lifetime of chronic hay fever and allergies. The nails dropped, fluttering from his fingers, rendering the digits enormously delicate and over-sensitive to even the slightest jarring...in a word, useless. Paralysis assailed his anal sphincter and the musty smell of feces rose as Todd fouled himself, an occurrence he would repeat innumerably until the end of his miserable, but—by Travis' intervention—astoundingly long life. Weeping sores inundated his groin and the toes of his left foot atrophied and dropped off as syphilis and cripppledness added themselves to his growing list of ailments. An accelerated fit of glaucoma burst his left eye and all of his upper teeth abscessed in an incapacitating wave of pain. His kidneys failed, necessitating life-long dialysis and cancers began to gnaw his prostate and testicles. Praying vainly for death, Todd fell prostrate at Travis's feet and begged for mercy. Had he known with whom he was dealing, he would have forgone the effort.

Two blocks away, in the rancid confines of Todd's

home, his children reeled as their individual IQs rose by some 200 points. The elder child bathed and dressed himself before dialing 911 and recounting to a horrified operator an epic tale of abuse and neglect. The operator immediately dispatched officers to arrest both Todd and his wife, who had suddenly been stricken with debilitating uterine cramps.

The children would become wards of the state and attend school, where they would demonstrate superhuman intelligence. At 18 and 16 respectively, they would graduate, valedictorians of Ivy League colleges, before attaining PhD's in cellular biology. The eldest would go on to discover a cure for cancer two months before his estranged father died of it in prison.

Chapter 35

Amazing Stunts at the Waterfront

The blue Ford Ranger glided inquisitively around dumpsters and slyly avoided the trappings of unpredictable one-way thoroughfares as it coursed to and fro in its nocturnal touring of the Seattle waterfront. Surly youths clad in the denim and flannel uniforms of the Northwest subculture, leered from the brightly lit confines of all-night fast food establishments, silently challenging the vagrants outside for dominion of the Emerald City's sleeping streets. Firefighters sipped black coffee and worked in their diligent, friendly way at raising a showroom finish from the tired, bloody pelt of a well-used hook and ladder. An engineer on one of the great, gently rumbling ferries, moored for a night of routine maintenance, took little notice of the crawling pickup as it negotiated the corner of Western and Madison, and came to a stop which, had it occurred eight hours prior, during the height of Seattle's rush hour, would have caused an automotive mishap of near gridlock proportions.

Matt, unsure of what exactly was transpiring in the steel blue shadows of that well-traveled intersection, stopped the Ranger and, against his better judgment, rolled down the tinted window for a better look. Hidden from the casual observer, but apparent to the inquisitive one, two vagrants, filthy, diseased and possessed of a monumental stench, masturbated one another in sporadic, jerking tempos between belts of a popular, alcohol-fortified citrus cordial. Matt's indiscreet headlights spilled across the intimate setting with curious effect. Distracted from their exercise by the unforeseen intrusion, the vagrants were frightened into emission and, inattentive to their aim, gave one another faces full of acrid semen. Tugging feverishly to extract the dregs of their lust, they turned in unison and cursed, "Get out of here, jackass. What are you, a faggot?" Embarrassed by both the situation and the ironic reprimand, Matt urged the Ford away in a squealing of tires that echoed between the sentinel skyscrapers before blending with and disappearing in the cries of startled gulls.

Crawling, moving without purpose on a seemingly random course, the Ranger and its sole occupant carried on in a weary effort to elude guilt and despair. Matt swore vehemently as compact discs suddenly spilled from their nylon carrying case and whispered across the floor mats. The maniacal leering of Iron Maiden's corpse-like mascot captured Matt's attention and he inserted the group's classic *Number of the Beast* album into the exquisite stereo system that was one of the Ranger's few amenities. Title track: A flurry of deft, yet forceful guitars out from which lyrics rose in an aggressive, surprisingly accomplished tenor.

"I left alone
my mind was blank.
I needed time to think
to get the memories from my mind.
What did I see?
Could I believe
that what I saw that night was real and not
just fantasy?
Just what I saw
in my own dreams
were the reflections of my woman staring
back at me.
Because in my dreams
it's always there,
the evil face that twists my mind and brings
me to despair."

The tenor rose in what could best be described as a "primal scale" and Matt, unaware that he had come to a stop in the middle of a street called Denny Way in the glow of the lights of an establishment called The Gentlemen's Club, relinquished his hold on the steering wheel and, hands clasped to his temples, began to weep.

Chapter 36

Amazing Grace

Grace Aarbogast, who for the next six hours would forfeit that name and assume the moniker and persona of "Ravenna," evened and blended the cosmetic foundation she had applied to hide the minuscule, but in her perception, screaming imperfections of her buttocks. Satisfied with her makeup, Ravenna composed herself and strode on six-inch chrome-tipped heels into the smoky spot-light of the Gentlemen's Club's mirrored stage. Cheap Trick's "Big Eye's" pulsed from hidden, but doubtlessly immense speakers as Ravenna, cool and remote, glided smoothly about, shedding article after article of clothing to the great delight of all the assembled…save one. At the rear of the room, where shadow and indifference hid the more subversive transactions not uncommon to the Gentlemen's Club, a strikingly ugly man, the silhouette of his vast nose filling the space between the glints of his diamond earrings, complained loudly to a bouncer. "But I came to see Raul! What do you mean lady's nights are Tuesday and Saturday? Pia Jesu dominé Donna raes requiem!" He stood, tilted his head in defiance, and in condescending tones informed the bouncer that his business would, in the future, be taken else-where. He muttered something to himself about orthodon-tics and began repeating, "Hector… Hector will help me." He flitted out the establishment's emergency exit, setting off a barrage of piercing alarms, and was nearly run down by a Ford Ranger which swerved at the last possible moment and struck a vagrant before careening into a park-ing space in the Gentlemen's Club's glass littered lot. The indignant patron genuflected before the mortally wounded vagrant, produced a host from his purse, and holding it before the bum's pain contorted face, recited, "Body of Christ," before lovingly running his tongue over the wafer and stuffing it back into his handbag. An ugly amalgam of blood and Night Train spilled from the broken vagrant's toothless face as his impeded faculties registered the sever-ity of the sacrilege he'd been forced to witness. "You should come with me, my son, to visit Hector… Hector makes everything better," the stranger cooed before rising and prancing on suede clogs into the waiting night.

Ravenna writhed and undulated with renewed vigor as the half gram of cocaine in which she'd indulged prior to the evening's first performance began to work its gregarious, extroverted magic. She arched and extended, stretched and spread in a practiced display of erotica that won the attention of even the most jaded old lesbians in the diverse audience. So intriguing was her performance that none saw the handsome, yet sad and distant, young man enter the room and advance, until he stood at the edge of the mirrored stage upon which Ravenna delighted. Intoxicating, amorous smells effused from the dancing girl; fragrances of perfume, hair spray, cosmetics and hosiery mingled in the air about her in a potpourri that heightened Matt's awareness for one deliciously fleeting moment and then...only darkness and seething dreams.

It was not until the young man at the foot of the stage swooned and fell limp to the semen-splattered floor that Ravenna took any real notice of him. She had no intention of interrupting her act, which was, by her own accounting, not to mention the enthusiastic concurrence of the assembled, going exceptionally well. *Piss on him. Probably drunk,* she thought to herself, before spinning a dizzying series of revolutions around the brass pole at center stage. As she negotiated a truly acrobatic dismount, and came to rest in Broadway quality splits, Ravenna saw, through the lingering remnants of pole-induced dizziness, a sight that led her, initially, to question the quality of the drugs her employer was providing. Before her, swaying pendulously from side to side, was...yes...it was a phallus of impossibly enormous size. The same crowd that had, only moments ago, teetered on the ragged brink of enthusiastic frenzy, lapsed into mute reverence at the spectacle of ponderous genitalia that unfurled before them. Enthralled beyond fear,  Ravenna tentatively extended a lace-gloved hand toward the turgid totem. Her tongue played involuntarily over the fullness of her painted lips, which suddenly dropped apart, disgorging an incensed scream as the erection eloquently addresses her, quoting Pliny, "Lust is an enemy to the purse, a foe to the person, a canker to the mind, a corrosive to the conscience, a weakness of the wit, a besotter of the senses and finally, a mortal bane to all the body." Comprehending none of the latter, Ravenna was left to conclude that the immensity before her was nothing more than a hologram— a scientific marvel of which she had read in *Seventeen* magazine. She wheeled 180 degrees, fatally discounting the threat represented by the serpentine phallus, and inadvertently offered her Esteé Lauder retouched buttocks to the silver-tongued titan which, accepting them wholeheartedly, brought her shift to a premature end.

Chapter 37

Discipline That Child

T he lullaby hymn of free air conditioning and the soft clinking of melting ice cubes played like a symphony of whispers in Will's half-heeding ears, driving him deeper and deeper into a dream of unparalleled bliss.

Julia Child, naked, excepting an adult (fat-assed) sized, disposable diaper and leather choker, pedaled a gleaming red tricycle in mad revolutions around "Ring Master Will." In his left hand, the Ring Master held a long, nylon leash, the opposite end of which was affixed to Julia's choker. In his right, he brandished a slender, but wickedly purposeful whip, which he wielded with uncanny skill at the torturous expense of Julia's generous flanks. She howled in a lamentable mezzo soprano under the implement's caresses and reluctantly disclosed her most closely guarded culinary secrets to Will, whose scribe, an eyeless baboon with huge, tattooed testicles, recorded them feverishly with a black pinstriped IBM Selectric typewriter. The machine's manufacturer's insignia had been modified in a crude attempt to establish a record of ownership and appeared as follows...

         I   B   M
         n   l   a
         t   i   n
         e   n   d
         l   d   r
         l   i
         i   l
         g   l
         e
         n
         t

The common denominator in all of the recipes thus far extracted had been copious amounts of sherry, rum, brandy, cognac, vermouth or any number of other potent distillates. The dream turned, without warning, into a nightmare, when the baboon, unable to reestablish the location of the typewriter's home keys after scratching its wiry pelt, had recorded a delicious sounding duck entrée as four paragraphs of "yjr fivl od yjrn yslrm smf omdrtyrf omyp s 690frhtrr pbrm smf nsfrf imyo; oy od pg sy ;rsdy rmrm vp;pt/" Disgusted with the creature's incompetence, Will turned his whip on the scholarly simian in a convincing display of negative reinforcement. Bloodlust smote the Ring Master, and he became so engrossed in the animal's attempts to penitently install a new correction ribbon, that he failed to notice Julia reaching into her great billowing diaper and producing a silver flask of high proof rum. Dousing herself with the liquor, she pedaled madly toward the admonished ape, whose typewriter she stole and crushed over her head in a desperate attempt to coax a spark from its innards. Her hopes realized, she burst into a scurrying meteorite of flame and vulgarity that streaked headlong into a huge, peripheral food processor and was julienned.

    The wail of police sirens roused Will from the disturbing dream. He rose, donned one of the terrycloth robes housekeeping kept the closets stocked with, and made his

179

DOC SOLOMMEN

way to the hotel room's expansive window wall just in time to see a set of tell-tale, blue flashing lights moving east on Denny Way. "And where in the hell is Matt?" he wondered pulling the heavy drapes together and renewing the darkness.

Chapter 38

Ambiance

Matt felt the far-off urging of his conscious mind and reluctantly opened his eyes. Darkness, and the sense of not being alone, surrounded him. He checked his temples and, secure in the knowledge that his spectacles were still in his possession, attempted to ascertain his whereabouts and the nature of what felt, very much, like a predicament. A voice in the darkness quoted Moore, "This wretched brain gave way, and I became a wreck, at random driven without one glimpse of reason, or of heaven." Matt leapt up in stark horror and dashed himself nearly unconscious on the steel dumpster lid which flew open with a hollow *gong* sound. A cold infusion of mercury vapor and moonlight flooded the trash receptacle's filthy confines. Surprised to find himself uninjured, save a handsome knot on his head, Matt crawled from the reeking dumpster, picking bits of refuse from his curiously tattered clothing. His shirt was intact, filthy, but intact. The front of his trousers was, however, reprehensibly devastated. He traced a greasy finger around the ragged aperture that existed in the space once occupied by his fly, and marveled at what appeared to be a dusting of cosmetic powder.

Instinct sent Matt scampering behind the hulking dumpster as the prying beam of a police cruiser's search light crawled the brick wall just above his head. The probing spotlight sparked vague memories of hours past in Matt's muddled mind. The circle jerking vagrants, the glitz of the nude bar…the girl. "My God, the girl," he moaned beneath his breath. Along with the memory of sweet Ravenna's gyrating charms came a repeated relinquishment of consciousness and resurrection of the mysterious orator he knew from dreams past—this time quoting Hannah Moore, "'A Christian will find it cheaper to pardon than to resent. Forgiveness saves the expense of anger, the cost of hatred, the waste of spirits.' Seek confession boy. Seek the sacrament." In lurching fits, Matt commenced his ascent of the Madison Street hill. He dragged himself eastward, toward St. James cathedral and its multitude of darkened confessionals.

Chapter 39

Silly Willy

The curtain's gentle billowing had given him the idea. Unable to sleep in the aftermath of the troubling dream, Will lay, contemplative and detached, sipping the sub-standard brew the in-room coffee maker had vomited up. Four full cups of the tan rot, unimproved by the addition of numerous packs of sugar, had passed his lips and was beginning to strain his bladder.

Having considered the circumstances, pondered the liability issue, and come to terms with himself on both accounts, Will rose and moved to stand at the foot of the room's second bed. He spent a moment assessing the queen's undisturbed sheets before pulling back the vulgar comforter. Nestling himself snugly into what should have been, had he chosen to stay, Matt's bed, Will (for the first and only time in his adult life) enjoyed a carefree pissing of the linens. A broad smile of sincere satisfaction played the corners of his boyish features and, for just a moment, he considered shitting the bed as well. He decided against it, however, and rising triumphantly, made his way to the shower.

Chapter 40

Gearing Up For Shutting Down

Will reluctantly checked out of the Hotel de Parvo, oblivious of the sidelong looks shot at him by the desk clerk, an attractive girl in her own right and a close friend of the housekeeper who had incurred the unenviable task of setting right Will's fouled linens. "Thank you sir, come again," she endeavored, the latter part of the formality falling from her demure lips with marked insincerity. As he gathered up his travel bags and turned from the desk, Will's eyes were drawn to a small gathering of hotel guests and employees who vied hotly for opportunities to view the striking show-bill displayed on the "Events and Information" board. "Critics call *Gomorra* cryptic, esoteric, and surreal… Wilson is mesmerizingly obtuse." Such were the venerations splattered over the original, horrifically shocking and irreverent art work that had been held over from the original printing.

Wilson's biblical masterpiece had taken the worlds of art, music and religion by storm. The Catholic church, along with the rest of the religious right, had condemned the work, forbidding its faithful to attend performances or purchase soundtracks—a maneuver that had propelled ticket sales and recording revenues to stratospheric heights. Wilson had appeared on the covers of several nationally distributed periodicals dressed in the bell bottom jump suit and leather platform shoes his opera had ushered back into mainstream fashion. The *Life* magazine cover for which he'd posed was, perhaps, the most remarkable. In striking black and white, Wilson, adorned in the robes of Christ, was depicted lashing a side of beef suspended from an evil-looking meat hook, with an equally vile looking cat-o-nine tails. Dangling from a bevy of additional hooks was the host of obese divas featured in *Gomorra's* first act. These were costumed in the solemn black and gray garb of Diocesan nuns. The stout sisters' expressions eloquently expressed their pent up lust for their lashing Lord and their hunger for a taste of his singing whip. Scribed in flowing text beneath the scandalous photo, the caption, "Lord have mercy!" completed the outrage. The issue surpassed even the 1963 Kennedy assassination memorial issue in sales, and of all the publications Wilson graced during his long overdue time of triumph, the *Life* cover was the one that hung, encased in acrylic, over his mantel through all of the bountiful years that followed.

Will's single word expressed the depth of his infatuation with the lewd show bill. "Whoa." His next $50 was happily exchanged, after a 90-minute wait in an impossibly long line, for a balcony seat ticket to that evening's performance of *Gomorra*. The wait had, at least, been made amusing by the carryings-on of a haughty transvestite with an elephantine nose, who openly gaped at explicit pictorials in a gay porno magazine he had brought with him to whittle away the time. Unknown to Will or the preoccupied pervert, their slow forward progress was being closely monitored from the rear of the line where, in the guise of a simple, civilian patron of the arts, the covert Father Vivian stood with his $50 in hand.

Chapter 41

A Night at the Opera

Attendance had risen steadily until the demand for tickets necessitated additional performances. The cast and crew of *Gomorra* had responded to the challenge with a professional zeal that thrilled Wilson and completed the spiritual circle of creator, performer and spectator. The energy that flowed through this ethereal circuit gave rise to increasingly brilliant performances until the opera's mean level of artistic execution reached a point as close to perfection as even Wilson could demand. The show's tenure at the Seattle Opera House had been extended indefinitely and the trades were heralding *Gomorra* as the *Tommy* of its time—a labeling Wilson vehemently opposed and tirelessly contradicted whenever the opportunity arose.

That night's performance was to mark the 100th time the spectacle of *Gomorra* would play, and the show had been billed, "Standing room only." Wilson, who was characteristically sullen and withdrawn prior to important performances, chatted freely with his cast members as they milled about the backstage area in the friendly chaos typical of the last minutes preceding the curtain's rising. The incessant lifting and falling of voices in tedious vocal scales, punctuated by the ponies' merry flatulence, lent a carnival atmosphere to the scene, and all but drowned out Wilson's shrill cry of, "Places everyone. Places!"

The orchestra, under Wilson's conduct, eased into the opera's hypnotic overture, and the cast knew, by the thunderous ovation, the precise moment Wilson's hydraulic dais lifted him up through the stage floor and into the harsh focus of the crowd's adoration. The venerable opera house

186

TRYPTOPHAN

was shaken to its very foundations as wave after wave of unrestrained worship crashed around the small figure of Wilson standing, godlike, on his pulpit. The tumultuous exultation would surely have gone on indefinitely had Wilson not called for and received capitulation. He stood in the breathless silence, arms upraised, baton at the ready.

Chapter 42

Act Three

The curtain rose on the third and final scene of history's most brazen opera. A steam shovel, its bulk gilded in gold leaf, lumbered out from stage left and clanked its way into the white spotlight where it shone like a great jewel held before the sun. Those scant portions of the machine's metallic hide not bedecked in shimmering gold were alive with faithful recreations of Michaelangelo's most inspired religious images. The tracks of the shining suropod were hidden from sight by a heavy curtain of embroidered velvet that rippled and swayed like a great regal kilt about the contraption's considerable girth. Standing in the leviathan's pure silver shovel, the bare-chested Christ, arms outstretched in a gesture of unconditional acceptance, presented himself to the swooning audience. The whole of the biblical monstrosity moved under the deft touch of Saints Peter and James, who co-occupied its jeweled cab and, along with the remaining ten apostles (all of whom hung and swung from numerous hand holds along the titan's flanks) sang a beautiful song of praise to their beloved master. The stage floor had been made to resemble a contemporary cemetery, and the sanctified steam shovel ground to a halt at its precise center. The great boom extended at St. Peter's control, and carried Christ out over the main floor audience, bringing him face to face with those fortunate few occupying the first balcony's front row seats. A very real, indeed, a nearly tangible religious awe descended over those in closest proximity to the crooning Christ as he sang, in a crystalline tenor, the first of his many arias:

Send forth all the sick to me
from Palestine, to Galilee
I'll cure the blind
I'll raise the dead
I'll make the cripple leap from bed
My Godly gift (My specialty)
is rectifying leprosy
I've worked the Jordan
shore to shore
clearing up those weeping sores—
So step up now
I'm thirty-one
I've got two years
before I'm done
please don't delay
I've seen the boss
and two years hence
(What tragic loss)
he's gonna hang me on a cross
but then, he's God
and that's his plan
so how can I help you, young man?

It took Matt an agonizingly long moment to realize and come to terms with the fact that the music had stopped and Christ was pointing at him...*him!* Before he could stop himself, Matt had blurted out his entire miserable story to the sympathetic savior, who nodded attentively as he took in the whole of the lad's tragedy. As his sobering tale came to an end, Matt's eyes filled with tears, then rolled back in black unconsciousness. His lithe frame convulsed grotesquely and, after a moment, Matt fell limply across his seat. Christ stood by benignly, the slightest look of annoyance clouding his benevolent face as Matt's denim trousers exploded and the hulk of his unnatural manhood rose up, swaying like an enraged cobra.

On the opposite side of the auditorium, Stanley's mascara-smudged eyes grew wide with unmitigated lust behind his mother of pearl opera glasses. He produced from his handbag a delicate lace fan and attempted to cool himself. The occupants of the seats adjacent Stanley's gaped in disgusted horror as his painted lips twitched and slackened, allowing shimmering rivulets of drool to run into the lap of his suede skirt, where they trickled down the sloping sides of a most inappropriate protrusion and formed languid pools on his thighs.

Christ extended his right arm in benediction and dispensed the blessing of the one true God onto the seething mass of Matt's serpentine penis, which reeled and undulated, contorting in desperation as it attempted to elude the sanctified touch. Driven beyond its ability to maintain a dignified silence, the organ wailed out Emerson, "The first lesson of history, is, that evil is good." The sound of stiletto heels clacking across the hardwood floor and shrill cries of, "Yes! Yes! Evil is my happy-happy!" emitted from the far side of the opera house as Stanley bolted from his seat and disappeared, in a primal monologue of senseless shrieking, down the aisle.

Christ motioned to his apostles and immediately, Saints Andrew and Thomas threw themselves from the steam shovel and began scouring the elaborate set for a handful or two of the rich, black dirt that had been used to lend realism to the stage dressings. Having found a suitable amount of the stuff, they signaled Saint Peter to swing the silver shovel and its load of Lord down to receive the hallowed handfuls.

Christ expectorated vigorously into the dark soil and proceeded to whip up a batch of luxurious mud, which he
slathered with abandon into the horrendous aperture at the
tip of Matt's vile penis. The gargantuan gland coiled itself
around Christ's wrist and, enraged, belched out Byron's,
"Hatred is the madness of the heart! Hatred is the madness
of the heart!"

The great double doors separating the opera house's
main auditorium from its opulent foyer swung open in utter
disdain for the epic struggle between good and evil that transpired beneath the lights. A hideous woman, possessed of a
hideously large nose and an equally hideous, saliva-smeared
suede skirt, loped moronically down the main aisle in the
direction of the stage. Before her eyes, she held a pair of
backward-turned opera glasses. Proceeding in drunken
lurches, she ascended the grand staircase that spiraled up to
the opera house's grand balcony, doggedly closing the gap
between herself and the pillar of animated flesh she seemed
to covet so desperately. Inverted as they were, the woman's
opera glasses left her under the impression that the object of
her desire was yet some distance away when, in actuality,
she had advanced to within mere inches of it. Ladies of style
and sophistication swooned and collapsed into the support-
ive arms of gentleman friends as the wailing woman misjudged her position relative to the railing, and sailed gracefully out over the balcony's edge. Continuing to ply her
determination to the motions of running, the ill-fated woman
continued along an arcing trajectory into one of the freshly
excavated graves over which the apostle-laden steam shovel
presided. As if composed to do so, the score paused an entire
measure, just enough time for a melodious fart to rise from
the freshly interred corpse, before continuing with renewed
vigor.

The apostles nodded their heads in enthusiastic approval
as Judas Iscariot was stitched into a remarkably life-like
cow suit and loaded, kicking and screaming in bovine

panic, into a box van whose stenciled door signage proudly declared it to be the property of the "Seattle Rendering Company."

Wretchedly gaunt pigs were herded across the stage by lesbian cowgirls who had attached to themselves, by means of elaborate harnesses, electrified, stainless steel phalli which they mercilessly employed to keep the herd moving. A fat sow strayed from the fold and was besieged by an enraged bull dyke who mounted the beast and unceremoniously forced her humming D.C.-powered dildo into the grunting animal's rectum. The house lights dimmed suddenly, and St. Elmo's fire crowned Wilson's swaying crop of hair as the ten kilowatt copulation reached its one-sided climax. When the lights finally came up, the exhausted lesbian was seen to be reclining in what appeared to be a shapeless, pink bean bag chair. She held a bleached pig skull in her hand and carried on in a distinctively Shakespearean vain while all around her, the delicious sound and smell of frying bacon rose to permeate the venue. St. James, the Lesser, was prompted to remind the audience that the consumption of the flesh of such animals that walk on cloven hooves was strictly forbidden.

Johnny Weismeuller, resurrected and luxuriously oiled, swung on a linen rope ornamented so as to resemble a jungle vine. He had abandoned the time-honored Tarzan call and sang Julio Inglesias numbers in its stead. The electrified lesbians, profoundly enraged at being upstaged by the upstart King of the Jungle, undertook the acrobatic venture of forming a pyramid in order to snatch Weismeuller from his vine and brutally sodomize him into silence. As the last cowgirl  ascended the mountainous heap of her sisters' bodies, however, she inadvertently touched her electrified dildo to that of one of her cohorts. The current of those two implements was multiplied in series, and in a reeking "woosh" of pyrotechnic ecstasy, the great pyramid melted into a seething, seafood buliobase. In an acrobatic move of his own, Weismeuller swung low and dragged his tongue through the bubbling puddle exclaiming, "You'll love it." He then swung a graceful arc upward, and disappeared from sight.

The combatant Christ donned a gi, and abandoning more traditional means of miracle working, delivered a series of vicious kicks to Matt's exposed testicles. The new tactic had swift and dramatic effect. Violent retching shook the leviathan, and in an unprecedentedly vulgar display of genital expulsion, the possessed penis vomited up the rotting remains of Hervé Villachez. The deceased dwarf straightened his smart bow tie and, brushing the remnants of his once handsomely feathered locks from empty eye sockets, proceeded to the precipice of the balcony's railing. He paused there a moment before executing a flawless pike into the yawning depths of one of the faux graves far below.

Antiquated iron lungs were wheeled onto the stage and creaked open to reveal wheezing Kentucky coal miners, all teetering on the brink of black lung oblivion. Wilson whipped the orchestra into a flurry of spirited blue grass music as the apostles provisioned the miners with French horns and beseeched them to make a joyful noise unto the Lord. Despite heroic individual efforts, the ramshackle brass section managed only a few pathetic grunts before collapsing, exhausted, into a grave beside Hervé.

Having disgorged the troublesome dwarf's remains, Matt's member shrank to its original proportions and lost all powers of speech and free will. It was, once again, just a dick. Alleviated of his mutated member's insatiable demand for blood, Matt's cardiovascular system was finally able to provide his brain and assorted viscera with the oxygen necessary for normal function. As if waking from a long sleep, Matt's consciousness returned with renewed clarity. Before him, borne aloft in a great sterling silver shovel and glistening with sweat in the white spot light, stood Jesus Christ. Extending his holy hand, Christ beckoned Matt to come forward.

A section of the opera house's great ceiling gave way. Amid a shower of concrete and tar roofing, a huge aircraft, stinking of barnyard offal and crimson with the spilled blood and matted wool of innumerable slain sheep, plummeted down, crashing horribly through the stage. Somewhere deep in the aircraft's wreckage, Deep Purple's "Highway Star" could be heard being sung in weak, but audible two-part harmony.

To the eternal wonder of all those assembled, a pristine ewe descended through the tattered roof. She was unblemished, as fresh as a gauze compress, and the light of divinity shined from her eyes. A beautiful, tranquil voice addressed the assemblage. "I am the lamb of God, who takes away the sins of the world. Happy are those who are called to my supper."

Travis leapt up from his front row seat and produced a cumbersome iron triangle from his designer tuxedo jacket. "Come and get it!" he bellowed, striking the triangle with a horrifyingly enormous pistol he'd subsequently drawn from a concealed holster. Shots rang out and, seconds later, the bullet-riddled corpse of the sanctified sheep lay impaled on a microphone stand at center stage. Blue sparks of static electricity arced between Wilson and the woolly interloper, and remained visible long after the house lights had faded to black.

Doc Solammen was born in Gary, Indiana on the downside of one of the more memorable decades of the 20th Century. Midwestern life disagreed with the Doctor, however, and in the high spring of 1987, he emigrated to Seattle in the hope that rain, and lots of it, would wash the residue of stockyards and steel mills from him. Whether or not he has been successful in this endeavor remains to be seen, but one thing is certain; between absolutions, the Doctor remains busy at his keyboard—a desperate man working frantically to exorcise the demons thrown up in the collision of his Catholic education with his Epicurean appetites.